CELT AND SAXON — COMPLETE
BY
George Meredith

CELT AND SAXON — COMPLETE

Published by Yurita Press

New York City, NY

First published circa 1909

Copyright © Yurita Press, 2015

All rights reserved

Except in the United States of America, this book is sold subject to the condition that it shall not, by way of trade or otherwise, be lent, re-sold, hired out, or otherwise circulated without the publisher's prior consent in any form of binding or cover other than that in which it is published and without a similar condition including this condition being imposed on the subsequent purchaser.

ABOUT YURITA PRESS

Yurita Press is a boutique publishing company run by people who are passionate about history's greatest works. We strive to republish the best books ever written across every conceivable genre and making them easily and cheaply available to readers across the world.

CHAPTER I. WHEREIN AN EXCURSION IS MADE IN A CELTIC MIND

A young Irish gentleman of the numerous clan O'Donnells, and a Patrick, hardly a distinction of him until we know him, had bound himself, by purchase of a railway-ticket, to travel direct to the borders of North Wales, on a visit to a notable landowner of those marches, the Squire Adister, whose family-seat was where the hills begin to lift and spy into the heart of black mountains. Examining his ticket with an apparent curiosity, the son of a greener island debated whether it would not be better for him to follow his inclinations, now that he had gone so far as to pay for the journey, and stay. But his inclinations were also subject to question, upon his considering that he had expended pounds English for the privilege of making the journey in this very train. He asked himself earnestly what was the nature of the power which forced him to do it—a bad genius or a good: and it seemed to him a sort of answer, inasmuch as it silenced the contending parties, that he had been the victim of an impetus. True; still his present position involved a certain outlay of money simply, not at all his bondage to the instrument it had procured for him, and that was true; nevertheless, to buy a ticket to shy it away is an incident so uncommon, that if we can but pause to dwell on the singularity of the act, we are unlikely to abjure our fellowship with them who would not be guilty of it; and therefore, by the aid of his reflections and a remainder of the impetus, Mr. Patrick O'Donnell stepped into a carriage of the train like any ordinary English traveller, between whom and his destination there is an agreement to meet if they can.

It is an experience of hesitating minds, be they Saxon or others, that when we have submitted our persons to the charge of public companies, immediately, as if the renouncing of our independence into their hands had given us a taste of a will of our own, we are eager for the performance of their contract to do what we are only half inclined to; the train cannot go fast enough to please us, though we could excuse it for breaking down; stoppages at stations are impertinences, and the delivery of us at last on the platform is an astonishment, for it is not we who have done it—we have not even desired it. To be imperfectly in accord with the velocity precipitating us upon a certain point, is to be going without our heads, which have so much the habit of supposing it must be whither we intend, when we go in a determined manner, that a doubt of it distracts the understanding—decapitates us; suddenly to alight, moreover, and find ourselves dropped at the heels of flying Time, like an unconsidered bundle, is anything but a reconstruction of the edifice. The natural revelry of the blood in speed suffers a violent shock, not to speak of our notion of being left behind, quite isolated and unsound. Or, if you insist, the condition shall be said to belong exclusively to Celtic nature, seeing that it had been drawn directly from a scion of one of those tribes.

Young Patrick jumped from the train as headless as good St. Denis. He was a juvenile thinker, and to discover himself here, where he both wished and wished not to be, now deeming the negative sternly in the ascendant, flicked his imagination with awe of the influence of the railway service upon the destinies of man. Settling a mental debate about a backward flight, he drove across the land so foreign to his eyes and affections, and breasted a strong tide of wishes that it were in a contrary direction. He would rather have looked upon the desert under a sand-storm, or upon a London suburb yet he looked thirstingly. Each variation of landscape of the curved highway offered him in a moment decisive features: he fitted them to a story he knew: the whole circle was animated by a couple of pale mounted figures beneath no happy light. For this was the air once breathed by Adiante Adister, his elder brother Philip's love and lost love: here she had been to Philip flame along the hill-ridges, his rose-world in the dust-world, the saintly in his earthly. And how had she rewarded him for that reverential love of her? She had forborne to kill him. The bitter sylph of the mountain lures men to climb till she winds them in vapour and leaves them groping, innocent of the red crags below. The delicate thing had not picked his bones: Patrick admitted it; he had seen his brother hale and stout not long back. But oh! she was merciless, she was a witch. If ever queen-witch was, she was the crowned one!

For a personal proof, now: he had her all round him in a strange district though he had never cast eye on her. Yonder bare hill she came racing up with a plume in the wind: she was over the long brown moor, look where he would: and vividly was she beside the hurrying beck where it made edges and chattered white. He had not seen, he could not imagine her face: angelic dashed with demon beauty, was his idea of the woman, and there is little of a portrait in that; but he was of a world where the elemental is more individual than the concrete, and unconceived of sight she was a recognised presence for the green-island brain of a youth whose manner of hating was to conjure her spirit from the air and let fly his own in pursuit of her.

It has to be stated that the object of the youngster's expedition to Earlsfont was perfectly simple in his mind, however much it went against his nature to perform it. He came for the purpose of obtaining Miss Adister's Continental address; to gather what he could of her from her relatives, and then forthwith to proceed in search of her, that he might plead with her on behalf of his brother Philip, after a four years' division of the lovers. Could anything be simpler? He had familiarised himself with the thought of his advocacy during those four years. His reluctance to come would have been accountable to the Adisters by a sentiment of shame at his family's dealings with theirs: in fact, a military captain of the O'Donnells had in old days played the adventurer and charmed a maid of a certain age into yielding her hand to him; and the lady was the squire of Earlsfont's only sister: she possessed funded property. Shortly after the union, as one that has achieved the goal of enterprise, the gallant officer retired from the service nor did north-western England put much to his credit the declaration of his wife's pronouncing him to be the best of husbands. She naturally said it of him in eulogy; his own relatives accepted it in some contempt, mixed with a relish of his hospitality: his wife's were constant in citing his gain by the marriage. Could he possibly have been less than that? they exclaimed. An excellent husband, who might easily have been less than that, he was the most devoted of cousins, and the liberal expenditure of his native eloquence for the furtherance of Philip's love-suit was the principal cause of the misfortune, if misfortune it could subsequently be called to lose an Adiante.

The Adister family were not gifted to read into the heart of a young man of a fanciful turn. Patrick had not a thought of shame devolving on him from a kinsman that had shot at a mark and hit it. Who sees the shame of taking an apple from a garden of the Hesperides? And as England cultivates those golden, if sometimes wrinkled, fruits, it would have seemed to him, in thinking about it, an entirely lucky thing for the finder; while a question of blood would have fired his veins to rival heat of self-assertion, very loftily towering: there were Kings in Ireland: cry for one of them in Uladh and you will hear his name, and he has descendants yet! But the youth was not disposed unnecessarily to blazon his princeliness. He kept it in modest reserve, as common gentlemen keep their physical strength. His reluctance to look on Earlsfont sprang from the same source as unacknowledged craving to see the place, which had precipitated him thus far upon his road: he had a horror of scenes where a faithless girl had betrayed her lover. Love was his visionary temple, and his idea of love was the solitary light in it, painfully susceptible to coldair currents from the stories of love abroad over the world. Faithlessness he conceived to be obnoxious to nature; it stained the earth and was excommunicated; there could be no pardon of the crime, barely any for repentance. He conceived it in the feminine; for men are not those holy creatures whose conduct strikes on the soul with direct edge: a faithless man is but a general villain or funny monster, a subject rejected of poets, taking no hue in the flat chronicle of history: but a faithless woman, how shall we speak of her! Women, sacredly endowed with beauty and the wonderful vibrating note about the very mention of them, are criminal to hideousness when they betray. Cry, False! on them, and there is an instant echo of bleeding males in many circles, like the poor quavering flute-howl of transformed beasts, which at some remembering touch bewail their higher state. Those women are sovereignly attractive, too, loathsomely. Therein you may detect the fiend.

Our moralist had for some time been glancing at a broad, handsome old country mansion on the top of a wooded hill backed by a swarm of mountain heads all purple-dark under clouds flying thick to shallow, as from a brush of sepia. The dim silver of half-lighted lakewater shot along below the terrace. He knew the kind of sky, having oftener seen that than any other, and he knew the house before it was named to him and he had flung a discolouring thought across it. He contemplated it placably and studiously, perhaps because the shower-folding armies of the fields above likened its shadowed stillness to that of his Irish home. There had this woman lived! At the name of Earlsfont she became this witch, snake, deception. Earlsfont was the title and summary of her black story: the reverberation of the word shook up all the chapters to pour out their poison.

CHAPTER II. MR. ADISTER

Mr. Patrick O'Donnell drove up to the gates of Earlsfont notwithstanding these emotions, upon which light matter it is the habit of men of his blood too much to brood; though it is for our better future to have a capacity for them, and the insensible race is the oxenish.

But if he did so when alone, the second man residing in the Celt put that fellow by and at once assumed the social character on his being requested to follow his card into Mr. Adister's library. He took his impression of the hall that had heard her voice, the stairs she had descended, the door she had passed through, and the globes she had perchance laid hand on, and the old mappemonde, and the severely-shining orderly regiment of books breathing of her whether she had opened them or not, as he bowed to his host, and in reply to, 'So, sir! I am glad to see you,' said swimmingly that Earlsfont was the first house he had visited in this country: and the scenery reminded him of his part of Ireland: and on landing at Holyhead he had gone off straight to the metropolis by appointment to meet his brother Philip, just returned from Canada a full captain, who heartily despatched his compliments and respects, and hoped to hear of perfect health in this quarter of the world. And Captain Con the same, and he was very flourishing.

Patrick's opening speech concluded on the sound of a short laugh coming from Mr. Adister.

It struck the young Irishman's ear as injurious and scornful in relation to Captain Con; but the remark ensuing calmed him:

'He has no children.'

'No, sir; Captain Con wasn't born to increase the number of our clan,' Patrick rejoined; and thought: By heaven! I get a likeness of her out of you, with a dash of the mother mayhap somewhere. This was his Puck-manner of pulling a girdle round about from what was foremost in his head to the secret of his host's quiet observation; for, guessing that such features as he beheld would be slumped on a handsome family, he was led by the splendid severity of their lines to perceive an illimitable pride in the man likely to punish him in his offspring, who would inherit that as well; so, as is the way with the livelier races, whether they seize first or second the matter or the spirit of what they hear, the vivid indulgence of his own ideas helped him to catch the right meaning by the tail, and he was enlightened upon a domestic unhappiness, although Mr. Adister had not spoken miserably. The 'dash of the mother' was thrown in to make Adiante, softer, and leave a loophole for her relenting.

The master of Earlsfont stood for a promise of beauty in his issue, requiring to be softened at the mouth and along the brows, even in men. He was tall, and had clear Greek outlines: the lips were locked metal, thin as edges of steel, and his eyes, when he directed them on the person he addressed or the person speaking, were as little varied by motion of the lids as eyeballs of a stone bust. If they expressed more, because they were not sculptured eyes, it was the expression of his high and frigid nature rather than any of the diversities pertaining to sentiment and shades of meaning.

'You have had the bequest of an estate,' Mr. Adister said, to compliment him by touching on his affairs.

'A small one; not a quarter of a county,' said Patrick.

'Productive, sir?'

"Tis a tramp of discovery, sir, to where bog ends and cultivation begins.'

'Bequeathed to you exclusively over the head of your elder brother, I understand.'

Patrick nodded assent. 'But my purse is Philip's, and my house, and my horses.'

'Not bequeathed by a member of your family?'

'By a distant cousin, chancing to have been one of my godmothers.'

'Women do these things,' Mr. Adister said, not in perfect approbation of their doings.

'And I think too, it might have gone to the elder,' Patrick replied to his tone.

'It is not your intention to be an idle gentleman?'

'No, nor a vagrant Irishman, sir.'

'You propose to sit down over there?'

'When I've more brains to be of service to them and the land, I do.'

Mr. Adister pulled the arm of his chair. 'The professions are crammed. An Irish gentleman owning land might do worse. I am in favour of some degree of military training for all gentlemen. You hunt?'

Patrick's look was, 'Give me a chance'; and Mr. Adister continued: 'Good runs are to be had here; you shall try them. You are something of a shot, I suppose. We hear of gentlemen now who neither hunt nor shoot. You fence?'

'That's to say, I've had lessons in the art.'

'I am not aware that there is now an art of fencing taught in Ireland.'

'Nor am I,' said Patrick; 'though there's no knowing what goes on in the cabins.'

Mr. Adister appeared to acquiesce. Observations of sly import went by him like the whispering wind.

'Your priests should know,' he said.

To this Patrick thought it well not to reply. After a pause between them, he referred to the fencing.

'I was taught by a Parisian master of the art, sir.'

'You have been to Paris?'

'I was educated in Paris.'

'How? Ah!' Mr. Adister corrected himself in the higher notes of recollection. 'I think I have heard something of a Jesuit seminary.'

'The Fathers did me the service to knock all I know into me, and call it education, by courtesy,' said Patrick, basking in the unobscured frown of his host.

'Then you are accustomed to speak French?' The interrogation was put to extract some balm from the circumstance.

Patrick tried his art of fence with the absurdity by saying: 'All but like a native.'

'These Jesuits taught you the use of the foils?'

'They allowed me the privilege of learning, sir.'

After meditation, Mr. Adister said: 'You don't dance?' He said it speculating on the' kind of gentleman produced in Paris by the disciples of Loyola.

'Pardon me, sir, you hit on another of my accomplishments.'

'These Jesuits encourage dancing?'

'The square dance—short of the embracing: the valse is under interdict.'

Mr. Adister peered into his brows profoundly for a glimpse of the devilry in that exclusion of the valse.

What object had those people in encouraging the young fellow to be a perfect fencer and dancer, so that he should be of the school of the polite world, and yet subservient to them?

'Thanks to the Jesuits, then, you are almost a Parisian,' he remarked; provoking the retort:

'Thanks to them, I've stored a little, and Paris is to me as pure a place as four whitewashed walls:' Patrick added: 'without a shadow of a monk on them.' Perhaps it was thrown in for the comfort of mundane ears afflicted sorely, and no point of principle pertained to the slur on a monk.

Mr. Adister could have exclaimed, That shadow of the monk! had he been in an exclamatory mood. He said: 'They have not made a monk of you, then.'

Patrick was minded to explain how that the Jesuits are a religious order exercising worldly weapons. The lack of precise words admonished him of the virtue of silence, and he retreated— with a quiet negative: 'They have not.'

'Then, you are no Jesuit?' he was asked.

Thinking it scarcely required a response, he shrugged.

'You would not change your religion, sir?' said Mr. Adister in seeming anger.

Patrick thought he would have to rise: he half fancied himself summoned to change his religion or depart from the house.

'Not I,' said he.

'Not for the title of Prince?' he was further pressed, and he replied:

'I don't happen to have an ambition for the title of Prince.'

'Or any title!' interjected Mr. Adister, 'or whatever the devil can offer!—or,' he spoke more pointedly, 'for what fools call a brilliant marriage?'

'My religion?' Patrick now treated the question seriously and raised his head: 'I'd not suffer myself to be asked twice.'

The sceptical northern-blue eyes of his host dwelt on him with their full repellent stare.

The young Catholic gentleman expected he might hear a frenetic zealot roar out: Be off!

He was not immediately reassured by the words 'Dead or alive, then, you have a father!'

The spectacle of a state of excitement without a show of feeling was novel to Patrick. He began to see that he was not implicated in a wrath that referred to some great offender, and Mr. Adister soon confirmed his view by saying: 'You are no disgrace to your begetting, sir!'

With that he quitted his chair, and hospitably proposed to conduct his guest over the house and grounds.

CHAPTER III. CAROLINE

Men of the Adister family having taken to themselves brides of a very dusty pedigree from the Principality, there were curious rough heirlooms to be seen about the house, shields on the armoury walls and hunting-horns, and drinking-horns, and spears, and chain-belts bearing clasps of heads of beasts; old gold ornaments, torques, blue-stone necklaces, under glass-cases, were in the library; huge rings that must have given the wearers fearful fists; a shirt of coarse linen with a pale brown spot on the breast, like a fallen beech-leaf; and many sealed parchment-skins, very precious, for an inspection of which, as Patrick was bidden to understand, History humbly knocked at the Earlsfont hall-doors; and the proud muse made her transcripts of them kneeling. He would have been affected by these wonders had any relic of Adiante appeased his thirst. Or had there been one mention of her, it would have disengaged him from the incessant speculations regarding the daughter of the house, of whom not a word was uttered. No portrait of her was shown. Why was she absent from her home so long? where was she? How could her name be started? And was it she who was the sinner in her father's mind? But the idolatrous love between Adiante and her father was once a legend: they could not have been cut asunder. She had offered up her love of Philip as a sacrifice to it: Patrick recollected that, and now with a softer gloom on his brooding he released her from the burden of his grand charge of unfaithfulness to the truest of lovers, by acknowledging that he was in the presence of the sole rival of his brother. Glorious girl that she was, her betrayal of Philip had nothing of a woman's base caprice to make it infamous: she had sacrificed him to her reading of duty; and that was duty to her father; and the point of duty was in this instance rather a sacred one. He heard voices murmur that she might be praised. He remonstrated with them, assuring them, as one who knew, that a woman's first duty is her duty to her lover; her parents are her second thought. Her lover, in the consideration of a real soul among the shifty creatures, is her husband; and have we not the word of heaven directing her to submit herself to him who is her husband before all others? That peerless Adiante had previously erred in the upper sphere where she received her condemnation, but such a sphere is ladder and ladder and silver ladder high above your hair-splitting pates, you children of earth, and it is not for you to act on the verdict in decrying her: rather 'tis for you to raise hymns of worship to a saint.

Thus did the ingenious Patrick change his ground and gain his argument with the celerity of one who wins a game by playing it without an adversary. Mr. Adister had sprung a new sense in him on the subject of the renunciation of the religion. No thought of a possible apostasy had ever occurred to the youth, and as he was aware that the difference of their faith had been the main cause of the division of Adiante and Philip, he could at least consent to think well of her down here, that is, on our flat surface of earth. Up there, among the immortals, he was compelled to shake his head at her still, and more than sadly in certain moods of exaltation, reprovingly; though she interested him beyond all her sisterhood above, it had to be confessed.

They traversed a banqueting-hall hung with portraits, to two or three of which the master of Earlsfont carelessly pointed, for his guest to be interested in them or not as he might please. A reception-hall flung folding-doors on a grand drawing-room, where the fires in the grates went through the ceremony of warming nobody, and made a show of keeping the house alive. A modern steel cuirass, helmet and plume at a corner of the armoury reminded Mr. Adister to say that he had worn the uniform in his day. He cast an odd look at the old shell containing him when he was a brilliant youth. Patrick was marched on to Colonel Arthur's rooms, and to Captain David's, the sailor. Their father talked of his two sons. They appeared to satisfy him. If that was the case, they could hardly have thrown off their religion. Already Patrick had a dread of naming the daughter. An idea struck him that she might be the person who had been guilty of it over there on the Continent. What if she had done it, upon a review of her treatment of her lover, and gone into a convent to wait for Philip to come and claim her?—saying, 'Philip, I've put the knife to my father's love of me; love me double'; and so she just half swoons, enough to show how the dear angel looks in her sleep: a trick of kindness these heavenly women have, that we heathen may get a peep of their secret rose-enfolded selves; and dream 's no word, nor drunken, for the blessed mischief it works with us.

Supposing it so, it accounted for everything: for her absence, and her father's abstention from a mention of her, and the pretty good sort of welcome Patrick had received; for as yet it was unknown that she did it all for an O'Donnell.

These being his reflections, he at once accepted a view of her that so agreeably quieted his perplexity, and he leapt out of his tangle into the happy open spaces where the romantic things of life are as natural as the sun that rises and sets. There you imagine what you will; you live what you imagine. An Adiante meets her lover another Adiante, the phantom likeness of her, similar to the finger-tips, hovers to a meeting with some one whose heart shakes your manful frame at but a thought of it. But this other Adiante is altogether a secondary conception, barely descried, and chased by you that she may interpret the mystical nature of the happiness of those two, close-linked to eternity, in advance. You would learn it, if she would expound it; you are ready to learn it, for the sake of knowledge; and if you link yourself to her and do as those two are doing, it is chiefly in a spirit of imitation, in sympathy with the darting couple ahead....

Meanwhile he conversed, and seemed, to a gentleman unaware of the vaporous activities of his brain, a young fellow of a certain practical sense.

'We have not much to teach you in: horseflesh,' Mr. Adister said, quitting the stables to proceed to the gardens.

'We must look alive to keep up our breed, sir,' said Patrick. 'We're breeding too fine: and soon we shan't be able to horse our troopers. I call that the land for horses where the cavalry's well-mounted on a native breed.'

'You have your brother's notions of cavalry, have you!'

'I leave it to Philip to boast what cavalry can do on the field. He knows: but he knows that troopers must be mounted: and we're fineing more and more from bone: with the sales to foreigners! and the only chance of their not beating us is that they'll be so good as follow our bad example. Prussia's well horsed, and for the work it's intended to do, the Austrian light cavalry's a model. So I'm told. I'll see for myself. Then we sit our horses too heavy. The Saxon trooper runs headlong to flesh. 'Tis the beer that fattens and swells him. Properly to speak, we've no light cavalry. The French are studying it, and when they take to studying, they come to the fore. I'll pay a visit to their breeding establishments. We've no studying here, and not a scrap of system that I see. All the country seems armed for bullying the facts, till the periodical panic arrives, and then it 's for lying flat and roaring—and we'll drop the curtain, if you please.'

'You say we,' returned Mr. Adister. 'I hear you launched at us English by the captain, your cousin, who has apparently yet to learn that we are one people.'

'We 're held together and a trifle intermixed; I fancy it's we with him and with me when we're talking of army or navy,' said Patrick. 'But Captain Con's a bit of a politician: a poor business, when there's nothing to be done.'

'A very poor business!' Mr. Adister rejoined,

'If you'd have the goodness to kindle his enthusiasm, he'd be for the first person plural, with his cap in the air,' said Patrick.

'I detest enthusiasm.

'You're not obliged to adore it to give it a wakener.

'Pray, what does that mean?'

Patrick cast about to reply to the formal challenge for an explanation.

He began on it as it surged up to him: 'Well, sir, the country that's got hold of us, if we 're not to get loose. We don't count many millions in Europe, and there's no shame in submitting to force majeure, if a stand was once made; and we're mixed up, 'tis true, well or ill; and we're stronger, both of us, united than tearing to strips: and so, there, for the past! so long as we can set our eyes upon something to admire, instead of a bundle squatting fat on a pile of possessions and vowing she won't budge; and taking kicks from a big foot across the Atlantic, and shaking bayonets out of her mob-cap for a little one's cock of the eye at her: and she's all for the fleshpots, and calls the rest of mankind fools because they're not the same: and so long as she can trim her ribands and have her hot toast and tea, with a suspicion of a dram in it, she doesn't mind how heavy she sits: nor that 's not the point, nor 's the land question, nor the potato crop, if only she wore the right sort of face to look at, with a bit of brightness about it, to show an idea inside striking alight from the day that's not yet nodding at us, as the tops of big mountains do: or if she were only braced and gallant, and cried, Ready, though I haven't much outlook! We'd be satisfied with her for a handsome figure. I don't know whether we wouldn't be satisfied with her for politeness in her manners. We'd like her better for a spice of devotion to alight higher up in politics and religion. But the key of the difficulty's a sparkle of enthusiasm. It's part business, and the greater part sentiment. We want a rousing in the heart of us; or else we'd be pleased with her for sitting so as not to overlap us entirely: we'd feel more at home, and behold her more respectfully. We'd see the policy of an honourable union, and be joined to you by more than a telegraphic cable. That's Captain Con, I think, and many like him.'

Patrick finished his airy sketch of the Irish case in a key signifying that he might be one among the many, but unobtrusive.

'Stick to horses!' observed Mr. Adister.

It was pronounced as the termination to sheer maundering.

Patrick talked on the uppermost topic for the remainder of their stroll.

He noticed that his host occasionally allowed himself to say, 'You Irish': and he reflected that the saying, 'You English,' had been hinted as an offence.

He forgot to think that he had possibly provoked this alienation in a scornfully proud spirit. The language of metaphor was to Mr. Adister fool's froth. He conceded the use of it to the Irish and the Welsh as a right that stamped them for what they were by adopting it; and they might look on a country as a 'she,' if it amused them: so long as they were not recalcitrant, they were to be tolerated, they were a part of us; doubtless the nether part, yet not the less a part for which we are bound to exercise a specially considerate care, or else we suffer, for we are sensitive there: this is justice but the indications by fiddle-faddle verbiage of anything objectionable to the whole in the part aroused an irritability that speedily endued him with the sense of sanity opposing lunacy; when, not having a wide command of the undecorated plain speech which enjoyed his approval, he withdrew into the entrenchments of contempt.

Patrick heard enough to let him understand why the lord of Earlsfont and Captain Con were not on the best of terms. Once or twice he had a twinge or suspicion of a sting from the tone of his host, though he was not political and was of a mood to pity the poor gentleman's melancholy state of solitariness, with all his children absent, his wife dead, only a niece, a young lady of twenty, to lend an air of grace and warmth to his home.

She was a Caroline, and as he had never taken a liking to a Caroline, he classed her in the tribe of Carolines. To a Kathleen, an Eveleen, a Nora, or a Bessy, or an Alicia, he would have bowed more cordially on his introduction to her, for these were names with portraits and vistas beyond, that shook leaves of recollection of the happiest of life—the sweet things dreamed undesiringly in opening youth. A Caroline awakened no soft association of fancies, no mysterious heaven and earth. The others had variously tinted skies above them; their features wooed the dream, led it on as the wooded glen leads the eye till we are deep in richness. Nor would he have throbbed had one of any of his favourite names appeared in the place of Caroline Adister. They had not moved his heart, they had only stirred the sources of wonder. An Eveleen had carried him farthest to imagine the splendours of an Adiante, and the announcement of the coming of an Eveleen would perchance have sped a little wild fire, to which what the world calls curiosity is frozenly akin, through his veins.

Mr. Adister had spoken of his niece Caroline. A lacquey, receiving orders from his master, mentioned Miss Adister. There was but one Miss Adister for Patrick. Against reason, he was raised to anticipate the possible beholding of her, and Caroline's entrance into the drawing-room brought him to the ground. Disappointment is a poor term for the descent from an immoderate height, but the acknowledgment that we have shot up irrationally reconciles even unphilosophical youth to the necessity of the fall, though we must continue sensible of a shock. She was the Miss Adister; and how, and why? No one else accompanied them on their march to the dinner-table. Patrick pursued his double task of hunting his thousand speculations and conversing fluently, so that it is not astonishing if, when he retired to his room, the impression made on him by this young Caroline was inefficient to distinguish her from the horde of her baptismal sisters. And she had a pleasant face: he was able to see that, and some individuality in the look of it, the next morning; and then he remembered the niceness of her manners. He supposed her to have been educated where the interfusion of a natural liveliness with a veiling retenue gives the title of lady. She had enjoyed the advantage of having an estimable French lady for her governess, she informed him, as they sauntered together on the terrace.

'A Protestant, of course,' Patrick spoke as he thought.

'Madame Dugue is a Catholic of Catholics, and the most honourable of women.'

'That I'll believe; and wasn't for proselytisms,' said he.

'Oh, no: she was faithful to her trust.'

'Save for the grand example!'

'That,' said Caroline, 'one could strive to imitate without embracing her faith.'

'There's my mind clear as print!' Patrick exclaimed. 'The Faith of my fathers! and any pattern you like for my conduct, if it's a good one.'

Caroline hesitated before she said: 'You have noticed my Uncle Adister's prepossession; I mean, his extreme sensitiveness on that subject.'

'He blazed on me, and he seemed to end by a sort of approval.'

She sighed. 'He has had cause for great unhappiness.'

'Is it the colonel, or the captain? Forgive me!'

Her head shook.

'Is it she? Is it his daughter? I must ask!'

'You have not heard?'

Oh! then, I guessed it,' cried Patrick, with a flash of pride in his arrowy sagacity. 'Not a word have I heard, but I thought it out for myself; because I love my brother, I fancy. And now, if you'll be so good, Miss Caroline, let me beg, it's just the address, or the city, or the country—where she is, can you tell me?—just whereabouts! You're surprised: but I want her address, to be off, to see her; I'm anxious to speak to her. It's anywhere she may be in a ring, only show me the ring, I'll find her, for I've a load; and there's nothing like that for sending you straight, though it's in the dark; it acts like an instinct. But you know the clear address, and won't let me be running blindfold. She's on the Continent and has been a long time, and it was the capital of Austria, which is a Catholic country, and they've Irish blood in the service there, or they had. I could drop on my knees to you!'

The declaration was fortunately hushed by a supplicating ardour, or Mr. Adister would have looked more surprised than his niece. He stepped out of the library window as they were passing, and, evidently with a mind occupied by his own affairs, held up an opened letter for Caroline's perusal. She took a view of the handwriting.

'Any others?' she said.

'You will consider that one enough for the day,' was his answer.

Patrick descended the terrace and strolled by the waterside, grieved at their having bad news, and vexed with himself for being a stranger, unable to console them.

Half an hour later they were all three riding to the market-town, where Mr. Adister paid a fruitless call on his lawyer.

'And never is at home! never was known to be at home when wanted!' he said, springing back to the saddle.

Caroline murmured some soothing words. They had a perverse effect.

'His partner! yes, his partner is at home, but I do not communicate upon personal business with his partner; and by and by there will be, I suppose, a third partner. I might as well deposit my family history in the hands of a club. His partner is always visible. It is my belief that Camminy has taken a partner that he may act the independent gentleman at his leisure. I, meantime, must continue to be the mark for these letters. I shall expect soon to hear myself abused as the positive cause of the loss of a Crown!'

'Mr. Camminy will probably appear at the dinner hour,' said Caroline.

'Claret attracts him: I wish I could say as much of duty,' rejoined her uncle.

Patrick managed to restrain a bubbling remark on the respective charms of claret and duty, tempting though the occasion was for him to throw in a conversational word or two.

He was rewarded for listening devoutly.

Mr. Adister burst out again: 'And why not come over here to settle this transaction herself?—provided that I am spared the presence of her Schinderhannes! She could very well come. I have now received three letters bearing on this matter within as many months. Down to the sale of her hereditary jewels! I profess no astonishment. The jewels may well go too, if Crydney and Welvas are to go. Disrooted body and soul!—for a moonshine title!—a gaming-table foreign knave!—Known for a knave!—A young gentlewoman?—a wild Welsh...!'

Caroline put her horse to a canter, and the exclamations ended, leaving Patrick to shuffle them together and read the riddle they presented, and toss them to the wind, that they might be blown back on him by the powers of air in an intelligible form.

CHAPTER IV. THE PRINCESS

Dinner, and a little piano-music and a song closed an evening that was not dull to Patrick in spite of prolonged silences. The quiet course of things within the house appeared to him to have a listening ear for big events outside. He dreaded a single step in the wrong direction, and therefore forbore to hang on any of his conjectures; for he might perchance be unjust to the blessedest heroine on the surface of the earth—a truly awful thought! Yet her name would no longer bear the speaking of it to himself. It conjured up a smoky moon under confounding eclipse.

Who was Schinderhannes?

Mr. Adister had said, her Schinderhannes.

Patrick merely wished to be informed who the man was, and whether he had a title, and was much of a knave: and particularly Patrick would have liked to be informed of the fellow's religion. But asking was not easy.

It was not possible. And there was a barrel of powder to lay a fiery head on, for a pillow!

To confess that he had not the courage to inquire was as good as an acknowledgment that he knew too much for an innocent questioner. And what did he know? His brother Philip's fair angel forbade him to open the door upon what he knew. He took a peep through fancy's keyhole, and delighted himself to think that he had seen nothing.

After a turbulent night with Schinderhannes, who let him go no earlier than the opening of a December day, Patrick hied away to one of the dusky nooks by the lake for a bracing plunge. He attributed to his desire for it the strange deadness of the atmosphere, and his incapacity to get an idea out of anything he looked on: he had not a sensation of cold till the stinging element gripped him. It is the finest school for the cure of dreamers; two minutes of stout watery battle, with the enemy close all round, laughing, but not the less inveterate, convinced him that, in winter at least, we have only to jump out of our clothes to feel the reality of things in a trice. The dip was sharpening; he could say that his prescription was good for him; his craving to get an idea ceased with it absolutely, and he stood in far better trim to meet his redoubtable adversary of overnight; but the rascal was a bandit and had robbed him of his purse; that was a positive fact; his vision had gone; he felt himself poor and empty and rejoicing in the keenness of his hunger for breakfast, singularly lean. A youth despoiled of his Vision and made sensible by the activity of his physical state that he is a common machine, is eager for meat, for excess of whatsoever you may offer him; he is on the highroad of recklessness, and had it been the bottle instead of Caroline's coffee-cup, Patrick would soon have received a priming for a delivery of views upon the sex, and upon love, and the fools known as lovers, acrid enough to win the applause of cynics.

Boasting was the best relief that a young man not without modesty could find. Mr. Adister complimented him on the robustness of his habits, and Patrick 'would like to hear of the temptation that could keep him from his morning swim.'

Caroline's needle-thrust was provoked:

'Would not Arctic weather deter you, Mr. O'Donnell?' He hummed, and her eyes filled with the sparkle.

'Short of Arctic,' he had to say. 'But a gallop, after an Arctic bath, would soon spin the blood-upon an Esquimaux dog, of course,' he pursued, to anticipate his critic's remark on the absence of horses, with a bow.

She smiled, accepting the mental alertness he fastened on her.

We must perforce be critics of these tear-away wits; which are, moreover, so threadbare to conceal the character! Caroline led him to vaunt his riding and his shooting, and a certain time passed before she perceived that though he responded naturally to her first sly attacks, his gross exaggerations upon them had not been the triumph of absurdity she supposed herself to have evoked.

Her wish was to divert her uncle. Patrick discerned the intention and aided her.

'As for entertainment,' he said, in answer to Mr. Adister's courteous regrets that he would have to be a prisoner in the house until his legal adviser thought proper to appear, 'I'll be perfectly happy if Miss Caroline will give me as much of her company as she can spare. It's amusing to be shot at too, by a lady who's a good marksman! And birds and hares are always willing to wait for us; they keep better alive. I forgot to say that I can sing.'

'Then I was in the presence of a connoisseur last night,' said Caroline. Mr. Adister consulted his watch and the mantelpiece clock for a minute of difference between them, remarking that he was a prisoner indeed, and for the whole day, unless Camminy should decide to come. 'There is the library,' he said, 'if you care for books; the best books on agriculture will be found there. You can make your choice in the stables, if you would like to explore the country. I am detained here by a man who seems to think my business of less importance than his pleasures. And it is not my business; it is very much the reverse but I am compelled to undertake it as my own, when I abhor the business. It is hard for me to speak of it, much more to act a part in it.'

'Perhaps,' Caroline interposed hurriedly, 'Mr. O'Donnell would not be unwilling to begin the day with some duets?'

Patrick eagerly put on his shame-face to accept her invitation, protesting that his boldness was entirely due to his delight in music.

'But I've heard,' said he, 'that the best fortification for the exercise of the a voice is hearty eating, so I'll pay court again to that game-pie. I'm one with the pigs for truffles.'

His host thanked him for spreading the contagion of good appetite, and followed his example. Robust habits and heartiness were signs with him of a conscience at peace, and he thought the Jesuits particularly forbearing in the amount of harm they had done to this young man. So they were still at table when Mr. Camminy was announced and ushered in.

The man of law murmured an excuse or two; he knew his client's eye, and how to thaw it.

'No, Miss Adister, I have not breakfasted,' he said, taking the chair placed for him. 'I was all day yesterday at Windlemont, engaged in assisting to settle the succession. Where estates are not entailed!'

'The expectations of the family are undisciplined and certain not to be satisfied,' Mr. Adister carried on the broken sentence. 'That house will fall! However, you have lost no time this morning.—Mr. Patrick O'Donnell.'

Mr. Camminy bowed busily somewhere in the direction between Patrick and the sideboard.

'Our lawyers have us inside out, like our physicians,' Mr. Adister resumed, talking to blunt his impatience for a private discussion with his own.

'Surgery's a little in their practice too, we think in Ireland,' said Patrick.

Mr. Camminy assented: 'No doubt.' He was hungry, and enjoyed the look of the table, but the look of his client chilled the prospect, considered in its genial appearance as a feast of stages; having luminous extension; so, to ease his client's mind, he ventured to say: 'I thought it might be urgent.'

'It is urgent,' was the answer.

'Ah: foreign? domestic?'

A frown replied.

Caroline, in haste to have her duties over, that she might escape the dreaded outburst, pressed another cup of tea on Mr. Camminy and groaned to see him fill his plate. She tried to start a topic with Patrick.

'The princess is well, I hope?' Mr. Camminy asked in the voice of discretion. 'It concerns her Highness?'

'It concerns my daughter and her inheritance from her mad grandmother!' Mr. Adister rejoined loudly; and he continued like a retreating thunder: 'A princess with a title as empty as a skull! At best a princess of swamps, and swine that fight for acorns, and men that fight for swine!'

Patrick caught a glance from Caroline, and the pair rose together.

'They did that in our mountains a couple of thousand years ago,' said Mr. Camminy, 'and the cause was not so bad, to judge by this ham. Men must fight: the law is only a quieter field for them.'

'And a fatter for the ravens,' Patrick joined in softly, as if carrying on a song.

'Have at us, Mr. O'Donnell! I'm ashamed of my appetite, Miss Adister, but the morning's drive must be my excuse, and I'm bounden to you for not forcing me to detain you. Yes, I can finish breakfast at my leisure, and talk of business, which is never particularly interesting to ladies—though,' Mr. Camminy turned to her uncle, 'I know Miss Adister has a head for it.'

Patrick hummed a bar or two of an air, to hint of his being fanatico per la musica, as a pretext for their departure.

'If you'll deign to give me a lesson,' said he, as Caroline came away from pressing her lips to her uncle's forehead.

'I may discover that I am about to receive one,' said she.

They quitted the room together.

Mr. Camminy had seen another Miss Adister duetting with a young Irishman and an O'Donnell, with lamentable results to that union of voices, and he permitted himself to be a little astonished at his respected client's defective memory or indifference to the admonition of identical circumstances.

CHAPTER V. AT THE PIANO, CHIEFLY WITHOUT MUSIC

Barely had the door shut behind them when Patrick let his heart out: 'The princess?' He had a famished look, and Caroline glided along swiftly with her head bent, like one musing; his tone alarmed her; she lent him her ear, that she might get some understanding of his excitement, suddenly as it seemed to have come on him; but he was all in his hungry interrogation, and as she reached her piano and raised the lid, she saw it on tiptoe straining for her answer.

'I thought you were aware of my cousin's marriage.'

'Was I?' said Patrick, asking it of himself, for his conscience would not acknowledge an absolute ignorance. 'No: I fought it, I wouldn't have a blot on her be suspected. She's married! She's married to one of their princes!—married for a title!—and changed her religion! And Miss Adister, you're speaking of Adiante?'

'My cousin Adiante.'

'Well did I hate the name! I heard it first over in France. Our people wrote to me of her; and it's a name to set you thinking: Is she tender, or nothing like a woman,—a stone? And I put it to my best friend there, Father Clement, who's a scholar, up in everything, and he said it was a name with a pretty sound and an ill meaning—far from tender; and a bad history too, for she was one of the forty-nine Danaides who killed their husbands for the sake of their father and was not likely to be the fiftieth, considering the name she bore. It was for her father's sake she as good as killed her lover, and the two Adiantes are like enough: they're as like as a pair of hands with daggers. So that was my brother Philip's luck! She's married! It's done; it's over, like death: no hope. And this time it's against her father; it's against her faith. There's the end of Philip! I could have prophesied it; I did; and when they broke, from her casting him off—true to her name! thought I. She cast him off, and she couldn't wait for him, and there's his heart broken. And I ready to glorify her for a saint! And now she must have loved the man, or his title, to change her religion. She gives him her soul! No praise to her for that: but mercy! what a love it must be. Or else it's a spell. But wasn't she rather one for flinging spells than melting? Except that we're all of us hit at last, and generally by our own weapon. But she loved Philip: she loved him down to shipwreck and drowning: she gave battle for him, and against her father; all the place here and the country's alive with their meetings and partings:—she can't have married! She wouldn't change her religion for her lover: how can she have done it for this prince? Why, it's to swear false oaths!—unless it's possible for a woman to slip out of herself and be another person after a death like that of a love like hers.'

Patrick stopped: the idea demanded a scrutiny.

'She's another person for me,' he said. 'Here's the worst I ever imagined of her!—thousands of miles and pits of sulphur beyond the worst and the very worst! I thought her fickle, I thought her heartless, rather a black fairy, perched above us, not quite among the stars of heaven. I had my ideas. But never that she was a creature to jump herself down into a gulf and be lost for ever. She's gone, extinguished—there she is, under the penitent's hoodcap with eyeholes, before the faggots! and that's what she has married!—a burning torment, and none of the joys of martyrdom. Oh! I'm not awake. But I never dreamed of such a thing as this—not the hard, bare, lump-of-earth-fact:—and that's the only thing to tell me I'm not dreaming now.'

He subsided again; then deeply beseeching asked:

'Have you by chance a portrait of the gentleman, Miss Adister? Is there one anywhere?'

Caroline stood at her piano, turning over the leaves of a music-book, with a pressure on her eyelids. She was near upon being thrilled in spite of an astonishment almost petrifying: and she could nearly have smiled, so strange was his fraternal adoption, amounting to a vivification—of his brother's passion. He seemed quite naturally to impersonate Philip. She wondered, too, in the coolness of her alien blood, whether he was a character, or merely an Irish character. As to the unwontedness of the scene, Ireland was chargeable with that; and Ireland also, a little at his expense as a citizen of the polite world, relieved him of the extreme ridicule attached to his phrases and images.

She replied: 'We have no portrait.'

'May I beg to know, have you seen him?' said Patrick. Caroline shook her head.

'Is there no telling what he is like, Miss Adister?'

'He is not young.'

'An old man!'

She had not said that, and she wished to defend her cousin from the charge of contracting such an alliance, but Patrick's face had brightened out of a gloom of stupefaction; he assured her he was now ready to try his voice with hers, only she was to excuse a touch of hoarseness; he felt it slightly in his throat: and could he, she asked him, wonder at it after his morning's bath?

He vindicated the saneness of the bath as well as he was able, showing himself at least a good reader of music. On the whole, he sang pleasantly, particularly French songs. She complimented him, with an emphasis on the French. He said, yes, he fancied he did best in French, and he had an idea of settling in France, if he found that he could not live quietly in his own country.

'And becoming a Frenchman?' said Caroline.

'Why not?' said he. 'I'm more at home with French people; they're mostly of my creed; they're amiable, though they weren't quite kind to poor Lally Tollendal. I like them. Yes, I love France, and when I'm called upon to fix myself, as I suppose I shall be some day, I shan't have the bother over there that I should find here.'

She spoke reproachfully: 'Have you no pride in the title of Englishman?'

'I'm an Irishman.'

'We are one nation.'

'And it's one family where the dog is pulled by the collar.'

There was a retort on him: she saw, as it were, the box, but the lid would not open to assist her to it, and she let it go by, thinking in her patriotic derision, that to choose to be likened to the unwilling dog of the family was evidence of a want of saving pride.

Besides, she could not trust to the glibness of her tongue in a contest with a young gentleman to whom talking was as easy as breathing, even if sometimes his volubility exposed him to attack. A superior position was offered her by her being silent and critical. She stationed herself on it: still she was grieved to think of him as a renegade from his country, and she forced herself to say: 'Captain O'Donnell talks in that manner.'

'Captain Con is constitutionally discontented because he's a bard by nature, and without the right theme for his harp,' said Patrick. 'He has a notion of Erin as the unwilling bride of Mr. Bull, because her lord is not off in heroics enough to please her, and neglects her, and won't let her be mistress of her own household, and she can't forget that he once had the bad trick of beating her: she sees the marks. And you mayn't believe it, but the Captain's temper is to praise and exalt. It is. Irony in him is only eulogy standing on its head: a sort of an upside down; a perversion: that's our view of him at home. All he desires is to have us on the march, and he'd be perfectly happy marching, never mind the banner, though a bit of green in it would put him in tune, of course. The banner of the Cid was green, Miss Adister: or else it's his pennon that was. And there's a quantity of our blood in Spain too. We've watered many lands.'

The poor young English lady's brain started wildly on the effort to be with him, and to understand whether she listened to humour or emotion: she reposed herself as well as she could in the contemplation of an electrically-flashing maze, where every line ran losing itself in another.

He added: 'Old Philip!' in a visible throb of pity for his brother; after the scrupulous dubitation between the banner and the pennon of the Cid!

It would have comforted her to laugh. She was closer upon tears, and without any reason for them in her heart.

Such a position brings the hesitancy which says that the sitting is at an end.

She feared, as she laid aside her music-books, that there would be more to come about Adiante, but he spared her. He bowed to her departing, and strolled off by himself.

CHAPTER VI. A CONSULTATION: WITH OPINIONS UPON WELSHWOMEN AND THE CAMBRIAN RACE

Later in the day she heard that he was out scouring the country on one of her uncle's horses. She had too many distressing matters to think of for so singular a young man to have any other place than that which is given to the fantastical in a troubled and serious mind. He danced there like the whimsy sunbeam of a shaken water below. What would be his opinion of Adiante if he knew of her determination to sell the two fair estates she inherited from a grandmother whom she had venerated; that she might furnish arms to her husband to carry out an audacious enterprise likely to involve both of them in blood and ruin? Would he not bound up aloft and quiver still more wildly? She respected, quaint though it was, his imaginative heat of feeling for Adiante sufficiently to associate him with her so far; and she lent him in fancy her own bewilderment and grief at her cousin's conduct, for the soothing that his exaggeration of them afforded her. She could almost hear his outcry.

The business of the hour demanded more of her than a seeking for refreshment. She had been invited to join the consultation of her uncle with his lawyer. Mr. Adister tossed her another letter from Vienna, of that morning's delivery. She read it with composure. It became her task to pay no heed to his loss of patience, and induce him to acquiesce in his legal adviser's view which was, to temporise further, present an array of obstacles, and by all possible suggestions induce the princess to come over to England, where her father's influence with her would have a chance of being established again; and it might then be hoped that she, who had never when under sharp temptation acted disobediently to his wishes at home, and who certainly would not have dreamed of contracting the abhorred alliance had she been breathing the air of common sense peculiar to her native land, would see the prudence, if not the solemn obligation, of retaining to herself these family possessions. Caroline was urgent with her uncle to act on such good counsel. She marvelled at his opposition, though she detected the principal basis of it.

Mr. Adister had no ground of opposition but his own intemperateness. The Welsh grandmother's legacy of her estates to his girl, overlooking her brothers, Colonel Arthur and Captain David, had excessively vexed him, despite the strong feeling he entertained for Adiante; and not simply because of the blow he received in it unexpectedly from that old lady, as the last and heaviest of the long and open feud between them, but also, chiefly, that it outraged and did permanent injury to his ideas of the proper balance of the sexes. Between himself and Mrs. Winnion Rhys the condition of the balance had been a point of vehement disputation, she insisting to have it finer up to equality, and he that the naturally lighter scale should continue to kick the beam. Behold now the consequence of the wilful Welshwoman's insanest of legacies! The estates were left to Adiante Adister for her sole use and benefit, making almost a man of her, and an unshackled man, owing no dues to posterity. Those estates in the hands of a woman are in the hands of her husband; and the husband a gambler and a knave, they are in the hands of the Jews—or gone to smoke. Let them go. A devilish malignity bequeathed them: let them go back to their infernal origin. And when they were gone, his girl would soon discover that there was no better place to come to than her home; she would come without an asking, and alone, and without much prospect of the intrusion of her infamous Hook-nose in pursuit of her at Earlsfont. The money wasted, the wife would be at peace. Here she would have leisure to repent of all the steps she had taken since that fatal one of the acceptance of the invitation to the Embassy at Vienna. Mr. Adister had warned her both against her going and against the influence of her friend Lady Wenchester, our Ambassadress there, another Welsh woman, with the weathervane head of her race. But the girl would accept, and it was not for him to hold out. It appeared to be written that the Welsh, particularly Welsh women, were destined to worry him up to the end of his days. Their women were a composition of wind and fire. They had no reason, nothing solid in their whole nature. Englishmen allied to them had to learn that they were dealing with broomstick witches and irresponsible sprites. Irishwomen were models of propriety beside them: indeed Irishwomen might often be patterns to their English sisterhood. Mr. Adister described the Cambrian ladies as a kind of daughters of the Fata Morgana, only half human, and deceptive down to treachery, unless you had them fast by their spinning fancy. They called it being romantic. It was the ante-chamber of madness. Mad, was the word for them. You pleased them you knew not how, and just as little did you know how you displeased them. And you were long hence to be taught that in a certain past year, and a certain month, and on a certain day of the month, not forgetting the hour of the day to the minute of the hour, and attendant circumstances to swear loud witness to it, you had mortally offended them. And you receive your blow: you are sure to get it: the one passion of those women is for vengeance. They taste a wound from the lightest touch, and they nurse the venom for you. Possibly you may in their presence have had occasion to praise the military virtues of the builder of Carnarvon Castle. You are by and by pierced for it as hard as they can thrust. Or you have incidentally compared Welsh mutton with Southdown:—you have not highly esteemed their drunken Bards:—you have asked what the Welsh have done in the world; you are supposed to have slighted some person of their family—a tenth cousin!—anything turns their blood. Or you have once looked straight at them without speaking, and you discover years after that they have chosen to foist on you their idea of your idea at the moment; and they have the astounding presumption to account this misreading of your look to the extent of a full justification, nothing short of righteous, for their treachery and your punishment! O those Welshwomen!

The much-suffering lord of Earlsfont stretched forth his open hand, palm upward, for a testifying instrument to the plain truth of his catalogue of charges. He closed it tight and smote the table. 'Like mother—and grandmother too—like daughter!' he said, and generalised again to preserve his dignity: 'They're aflame in an instant. You may see them quiet for years, but it smoulders. You dropped the spark, and they time the explosion.'

Caroline said to Mr. Camminy: 'You are sure you can give us the day?'

'All of it,' he replied, apologising for some show of restlessness. 'The fact is, Miss Adister, I married a lady from over the borders, and though I have never had to complain of her yet, she may have a finale in store. It's true that I love wild Wales.'

'And so do I' Caroline raised her eyes to imagined mountains.

'You will pardon me, Camminy,' said Mr. Adister.

The lawyer cracked his back to bow to the great gentleman so magnanimously humiliating himself. 'Sir! Sir!' he said. 'Yes, Welsh blood is queer blood, I own. They find it difficult to forgive; and trifles offend; and they are unhappily just as secretive as they are sensitive. The pangs we cause them, without our knowing it, must be horrible. They are born, it would seem, with more than the common allowance of kibes for treading on: a severe misfortune for them. Now for their merits: they have poetry in them; they are valiant; they are hospitable to teach the Arab a lesson: I do believe their life is their friend's at need—seriously, they would lay it down for him: or the wherewithal, their money, their property, excepting the three-stringed harp of three generations back, worth now in current value sixpence halfpenny as a curiosity, or three farthings for firewood; that they'll keep against their own desire to heap on you everything they have—if they love you, and you at the same time have struck their imaginations. Offend them, however, and it's war, declared or covert. And I must admit that their best friend can too easily offend them. I have lost excellent clients, I have never understood why; yet I respect the remains of their literature, I study their language, I attend their gatherings and subscribe the expenses; I consume Welsh mutton with relish; I enjoy the Triads, and can come down on them with a quotation from Catwg the Wise: but it so chanced that I trod on a kibe, and I had to pay the penalty. There's an Arabian tale, Miss Adister, of a peaceful traveller who ate a date in the desert and flung away the stone, which hit an invisible son of a genie in the eye, and the poor traveller suffered for it. Well, you commit these mortal injuries to the invisible among the Welsh. Some of them are hurt if you call them Welsh. They scout it as the original Saxon title for them. No, they are Cymry, Cambrians! They have forgiven the Romans. Saxon and Norman are still their enemies. If you stir their hearts you find it so. And, by the way, if King Edward had not trampled them into the mire so thoroughly, we should hear of it at times even now. Instead of penillions and englyns, there would be days for fiery triplets. Say the worst of them, they are soundheaded. They have a ready comprehension for great thoughts. The Princess Nikolas, I remember, had a special fondness for the words of Catwg the Wise.'

'Adiante,' had murmured Caroline, to correct his indiscretion.

She was too late.

'Nikolas!' Mr. Adister thundered. 'Hold back that name in this house, title and all, if you speak of my daughter. I refuse admission to it here. She has given up my name, and she must be known by the one her feather-brained grandmother proposed for her, to satisfy her pleasure in a fine sound. English Christian names are my preference. I conceded Arthur to her without difficulty. She had a voice in David, I recollect; with very little profit to either of the boys. I had no voice in Adiante; but I stood at my girl's baptism, and Adiante let her be. At least I saved the girl from the addition of Arianrod. It was to have been Adiante Arianrod. Can you credit it? Prince-pah! Nikolas? Have you a notion of the sort of prince that makes an English lady of the best blood of England his princess?'

The lawyer had a precise notion of the sort of prince appearing to Mr. Adister in the person of his foreign son-in-law. Prince Nikolas had been described to him before, with graphic touches upon the quality of the reputation he bore at the courts and in the gambling-saloons of Europe. Dreading lest his client's angry heat should precipitate him on the prince again, to the confusion of a lady's ears, Mr. Camminy gave an emphatic and short affirmative.

'You know what he is like?' said Mr. Adister, with a face of disgust reflected from the bare thought of the hideous likeness.

Mr. Camminy assured him that the description of the prince's lineaments would not be new. It was, as he was aware, derived from a miniature of her husband, transmitted by the princess, on its flight out of her father's loathing hand to the hearthstone and under his heel.

Assisted by Caroline, he managed to check the famous delineation of the adventurer prince in which a not very worthy gentleman's chronic fever of abomination made him really eloquent, quick to unburden himself in the teeth of decorum.

'And my son-in-law! My son-in-law!' ejaculated Mr. Adister, tossing his head higher, and so he stimulated his amazement and abhorrence of the portrait he rather wondered at them for not desiring to have sketched for their execration of it, alluringly foul as it was: while they in concert drew him back to the discussion of his daughter's business, reiterating prudent counsel, with a knowledge that they had only to wait for the ebbing of his temper.

'Let her be informed, sir, that by coming to England she can settle the business according to her wishes in one quarter of the time it would take a Commission sent out to her—if we should be authorised to send out one,' said Mr. Camminy. 'By committing the business to you, I fancy I perceive your daughter's disposition to consider your feelings: possibly to a reluctance to do the deed unsanctioned by her father. It would appear so to a cool observer, notwithstanding her inattention to your remonstrances.'

The reply was: 'Dine here and sleep here. I shall be having more of these letters,' Mr. Adister added, profoundly sighing.

Caroline slipped away to mark a conclusion to the debate; and Mr. Camminy saw his client redden fast and frown.

'Besides,' he spoke in a husky voice, descending upon a subject hateful, 'she tells me to-day she is not in a state to travel! Do you hear? Make what you can of it.'

The proud and injured gentleman had the aspect of one who receives a blow that it is impossible for him to resent. He could not speak the shame he felt: it was literally in his flesh. But the cause had been sufficiently hinted to set the lawyer staring as men do when they encounter situations of grisly humour, where certain of the passions of man's developed nature are seen armed and furious against our mild prevailing ancient mother nature; and the contrast is between our utter wrath and her simple exposition of the circumstances and consequences forming her laws. There are situations which pass beyond the lightly stirred perceptive wits to the quiet court of the intellect, to be received there as an addition to our acquaintance with mankind. We know not of what substance to name them. Humour in its intense strain has a seat somewhere about the mouth of tragedy, giving it the enigmatical faint wry pull at a corner visible at times upon the dreadful mask.

That Mr. Adister should be astonished at such a communication from the princess, after a year of her marriage: and that he should take it for a further outrage of his paternal sentiments, should actually redden and be hoarse in alluding to it: the revelation of such points in our human character set the humane old lawyer staring at the reserve space within himself apart from his legal being, whereon he by fits compared his own constitution with that of the individuals revealed to him by their acts and confidential utterances. For him, he decided that he would have rejoiced at the news.

Granting the prince a monster, however, as Mr. Adister unforcedly considered him, it was not so cheering a piece of intelligence that involved him yet closer with that man's rank blood: it curdled his own. The marriage had shocked and stricken him, cleaving, in his love for his daughter, a goodly tree and withering many flowers. Still the marriage was but Adiante's gulf: he might be called father-in-law of her spangled ruffian; son-in-law, the desperado-rascal would never be called by him. But the result of the marriage dragged him bodily into the gulf: he became one of four, numbering the beast twice among them. The subtlety of his hatred so reckoned it; for he could not deny his daughter in the father's child; he could not exclude its unhallowed father in the mother's: and of this man's child he must know and own himself the grandfather. If ever he saw the child, if drawn to it to fondle it, some part of the little animal not his daughter's would partake of his embrace. And if neither of his boys married, and his girl gave birth to a son! darkness rolled upon that avenue of vision. A trespasser and usurper-one of the demon's brood chased his very name out of Earlsfont!

'Camminy, you must try to amuse yourself,' he said briskly. 'Anything you may be wanting at home shall be sent for. I must have you here to make sure that I am acting under good advice. You can take one of the keepers for an hour or two of shooting. I may join you in the afternoon. You will find occupation for your gun in the north covers.'

He wandered about the house, looking into several rooms, and only partially at rest when he discovered Caroline in one, engaged upon some of her aquarelle sketches. He asked where the young Irishman was.

'Are you in search of him?' said she. 'You like him, uncle? He is out riding, they tell me.'

'The youngster is used to south-western showers in that climate of his,' Mr. Adister replied. 'I dare say we could find the Jesuit in him somewhere. There's the seed. His cousin Con O'Donnell has filled him with stuff about Ireland and England: the man has no better to do than to train a parrot. What do you think of him, my love?'

The judgement was not easily formed for expression. 'He is not quite like what I remember of his brother Philip. He talks much more, does he not? He seems more Irish than his brother. He is very strange. His feelings are strong; he has not an idea of concealing them. For a young man educated by the Jesuits, he is remarkably open.'

'The Jesuits might be of service to me just now!' Mr. Adister addressed his troubled soul, and spoke upon another conception of them: 'How has he shown his feelings?'

Caroline answered quickly: 'His love of his brother. Anything that concerns his brother moves him; it is like a touch on a musical instrument. Perhaps I should say a native one.'

'Concerns his brother?' Mr. Adister inquired, and his look requesting enlightenment told her she might speak.

'Adiante,' she said softly. She coloured.

Her uncle mused awhile in a half-somnolent gloom. 'He talks of this at this present day?'

'It is not dead to him. He really appears to have hoped... he is extraordinary. He had not heard before of her marriage. I was a witness of the most singular scene this morning, at the piano. He gathered it from what he had heard. He was overwhelmed by it. I could not exaggerate. It was impossible to help being a little touched, though it was curious, very strange.'

Her uncle's attentiveness incited her to describe the scene, and as it visibly relieved his melancholy, she did it with a few vivid indications of the quaint young Irishman's manner of speech. She concluded: 'At last he begged to see a portrait of her husband.'

'Not of her?' said Mr. Adister abruptly.

'No; only of her husband.'

'Show him her portrait.'

A shade of surprise was on Caroline's forehead. 'Shall I?' She had a dim momentary thought that the sight of the beautiful face would not be good for Patrick.

'Yes; let him see the woman who could throw herself away on that branded villain called a prince, abjuring her Church for a little fouler than hangman to me and every gentleman alive. I desire that he should see it. Submission to the demands of her husband's policy required it of her, she says! Show it him when he returns; you have her miniature in your keeping. And to-morrow take him to look at the full-length of her before she left England and ceased to be a lady of our country. I will order it to be placed in the armoury. Let him see the miniature of her this day.'

Mr. Adister resolved at the same time that Patrick should have his portrait of the prince for a set-off to the face of his daughter. He craved the relief it would be to him to lay his colours on the prince for the sparkling amazement of one whom, according to Caroline's description, he could expect to feel with him acutely, which neither his niece nor his lawyer had done: they never did when he painted the prince. He was unstrung, heavily plunged in the matter of his chagrin and grief: his unhealed wound had been scraped and strewn with salt by his daughter's letter; he had a thirst for the kind of sympathy he supposed he would find in the young Irishman's horror at the husband of the incomparable beauty now past redemption degraded by her hideous choice; lost to England and to her father and to common respect. For none, having once had the picture of the man, could dissociate them; they were like heaven and its reverse, everlastingly coupled in the mind by their opposition of characters and aspects. Her father could not, and he judged of others by himself. He had been all but utterly solitary since her marriage, brooded on it until it saturated him; too proud to speak of the thing in sadness, or claim condolence for this wound inflicted on him by the daughter he had idolised other than through the indirect method of causing people to wonder at her chosen yoke-fellow. Their stupefaction refreshed him. Yet he was a gentleman capable of apprehending simultaneously that he sinned against his pride in the means he adopted to comfort his nature. But the wound was a perpetual sickness needing soul-medicine. Proud as he was, and unbending, he was not stronger than his malady, and he could disguise, he could not contain, the cry of immoderate grief. Adiante had been to him something beyond a creature beloved; she had with her glorious beauty and great-heartedness been the sole object which had ever inspirited his imagination. He could have thought no man, not the most illustrious, worthy of her. And there she was, voluntarily in the hands of a monster! 'Husband!' Mr. Adister broke away from Caroline, muttering: 'Her husband's policy!'

She was used to his interjections; she sat thinking more of the strange request to her to show Mr. O'Donnell the miniature of Adiante. She had often thought that her uncle regretted his rejection of Philip. It appeared so to her now, though not by any consecutive process of reasoning. She went to fetch the miniature, and gazing on it, she tried to guess at Mr. O'Donnell's thoughts when doing the same; for who so inflammable as he? And who, woman or man, could behold this lighted face, with the dark raised eyes and abounding auburn tresses, where the contrast of colours was in itself thrilling, and not admire, or more, half worship, or wholly worship? She pitied the youth: she fancied that he would not continue so ingenuously true to his brother's love of Adiante after seeing it; unless one might hope that the light above beauty distinguishing its noble classic lines, and the energy of radiance, like a morning of chivalrous promise, in the eyes, would subdue him to distant admiration. These were her flitting thoughts under the spell of her queenly cousin's visage. She shut up the miniature-case, and waited to hand it to young Mr. O'Donnell.

CHAPTER VII. THE MINIATURE

Patrick returned to Earlsfont very late; he had but ten minutes to dress for dinner; a short allowance after a heated ride across miry tracks, though he would have expended some of them, in spite of his punctilious respect for the bell of the house entertaining him, if Miss Adister had been anywhere on the stairs or corridors as he rushed away to his room. He had things to tell; he had not been out over the country for nothing.

Fortunately for his good social principles, the butler at Earlsfont was a wary supervisor of his man; great guest or little guest; Patrick's linen was prepared for him properly studded; he had only to spring out of one suit into another; and still more fortunately the urgency for a rapid execution of the manoeuvre prevented his noticing a large square envelope posted against the looking-glass of his toilette-table. He caught sight of it first when pulling down his shirt-cuffs with an air of recovered ease, not to say genial triumph, to think that the feat of grooming himself, washing, dressing and stripping, the accustomed persuasive final sweep of the brush to his hair-crop, was done before the bell had rung. His name was on the envelope; and under his name, in smaller letters,

Adiante.

'Shall I?' said he, doing the thing he asked himself about doing tearing open the paper cover of the portrait of her who had flitted in his head for years unseen. And there she was, remote but present.

His underlip dropped; he had the look of those who bate breath and swarm their wits to catch a sound. At last he remembered that the summoning bell had been in his ears a long time back, without his having been sensible of any meaning in it. He started to and fro. The treasure he held declined to enter the breast-pocket of his coat, and the other pockets he perhaps, if sentimentally, justly discarded as being beneath the honour of serving for a temporary casket. He locked it up, with a vow to come early to rest. Even then he had thoughts whether it might be safe.

Who spoke, and what they uttered at the repast, and his own remarks, he was unaware of. He turned right and left a brilliant countenance that had the glitter of frost-light; it sparkled and was unreceptive. No wonder Miss Adister deemed him wilder and stranger than ever. She necessarily supposed the excess of his peculiarities to be an effect of the portrait, and would have had him, according to her ideas of a young man of some depth of feeling, dreamier. On the contrary, he talked sheer commonplace. He had ridden to the spur of the mountains, and had put up the mare, and groomed and fed her, not permitting another hand to touch her: all very well, and his praises of the mare likewise, but he had not a syllable for the sublime of the mountains. He might have careered over midland flats for any susceptibility that he betrayed to the grandeur of the scenery she loved. Ultimately she fancied the miniature had been overlooked in his hurry to dress, and that he was now merely excited by his lively gallop to a certain degree of hard brightness noticeable in hunting men at their dinner.

The elixir in Patrick carried him higher than mountain crests. Adiante illumined an expanded world for him, miraculous, yet the real one, only wanting such light to show its riches. She lifted it out of darkness with swift throbs of her heavenliness as she swam to his eyelids, vanished and dazzled anew, and made these gleams of her and the dark intervals his dream of the winged earth on her flight from splendour to splendour, secresy to secresy;—follow you that can, the youth whose heart is an opened mine, whose head is an irradiated sky, under the spell of imagined magical beauty. She was bugle, banner, sunrise, of his inmost ambition and rapture.

And without a warning, she fled; her features were lost; his power of imagining them wrestled with vapour; the effort contracted his outlook. But if she left him blind of her, she left him with no lessened bigness of heart. He frankly believed in her revelation of a greater world and a livelier earth, a flying earth and a world wealthier than grouped history in heroic marvels: he fell back on the exultation of his having seen her, and on the hope for the speedy coming of midnight, when the fountain of her in the miniature would be seen and drunk of at his full leisure, and his glorious elation of thrice man almost up to mounting spirit would be restored to make him worthy of the vision.

Meanwhile Caroline had withdrawn and the lord of Earlsfont was fretting at his theme. He had decided not to be a party in the sale of either of his daughter's estates: let her choose other agents: if the iniquity was committed, his hands would be clean of it. Mr. Adister spoke by way of prelude to the sketch of 'this prince' whose title was a lurid delusion. Patrick heard of a sexagenarian rake and Danube adventurer, in person a description of falcon-Caliban, containing his shagginess in a frogged hussar-jacket and crimson pantaloons, with hook-nose, fox-eyes, grizzled billow of frowsy moustache, and chin of a beast of prey. This fellow, habitually one of the dogs lining the green tables of the foreign Baths, snapping for gold all day and half the night, to spend their winnings in debauchery and howl threats of suicide, never fulfilled early enough, when they lost, claimed his princedom on the strength of his father's murder of a reigning prince and sitting in his place for six months, till a merited shot from another pretender sent him to his account. 'What do you say to such a nest of assassins, and one of them, an outcast and blackleg, asking an English gentleman to acknowledge him as a member of his family! I have,' said Mr. Adister, 'direct information that this gibbet-bird is conspiring to dethrone—they call it—the present reigning prince, and the proceeds of my daughter's estates are, by her desire—if she has not written under compulsion of the scoundrel—intended to speed their blood-mongering. There goes a Welshwoman's legacy to the sea, with a herd of swine with devils in them!'

Mr. Camminy kept his head bent, his hand on his glass of port. Patrick stared, and the working of his troubled brows gave the unhappy gentleman such lean comfort as he was capable of taking. Patrick in sooth was engaged in the hard attempt at the same time to do two of the most difficult things which can be proposed to the ingenuity of sensational youth: he was trying to excuse a respected senior for conduct that he could not approve, while he did inward battle to reconcile his feelings with the frightful addition to his hoard of knowledge: in other words, he sought strenuously to mix the sketch of the prince with the dregs of the elixir coming from the portrait of Adiante; and now she sank into obscurity behind the blackest of brushes, representing her incredible husband; and now by force of some natural light she broke through the ugly mist and gave her adored the sweet lines and colours of the features he had lost. There was an ebb and flow of the struggle, until, able to say to himself that he saw her clearly as though the portrait was in the palm of his hand, the battle of the imagination ceased and she was fairer for him than if her foot had continued pure of its erratic step: fairer, owing to the eyes he saw with; he had shaken himself free of the exacting senses which consent to the worship of women upon the condition of their possessing all the precious and the miraculous qualities; among others, the gift of an exquisite fragility that cannot break; in short, upon terms flattering to the individual devotee. Without knowing it he had done it and got some of the upholding strength of those noblest of honest men who not merely give souls to women—an extraordinary endowment of them—but also discourse to them with their souls.

Patrick accepted Adiante's husband: the man was her husband. Hideous (for there was no combating her father's painting of him), he was almost interesting through his alliance:—an example of how much earth the worshipper can swallow when he is quite sincere. Instead of his going under eclipse, the beauty of his lady eclipsed her monster. He believed in her right to choose according to her pleasure since her lover was denied her. Sitting alone by his fire, he gazed at her for hours and bled for Philip. There was a riddle to be answered in her cutting herself away from Philip; he could not answer it; her face was the vindication and the grief. The usual traverses besetting true lovers were suggested to him, enemies and slanders and intercepted letters. He rejected them in the presence of the beautiful inscrutable. Small marvel that Philip had loved her. 'Poor fellow' Patrick cried aloud, and drooped on a fit of tears.

The sleep he had was urgently dream-ridden to goals that eluded him and broadened to fresh races and chases waving something to be won which never was won, albeit untiringly pursued amid a series of adventures, tragic episodes; wild enthusiasm. The whole of it was featureless, a shifting agitation; yet he must have been endowed to extricate a particular meaning applied to himself out of the mass of tumbled events, and closely in relation to realities, for he quitted his bed passionately regretting that he had not gone through a course of drill and study of the military art. He remembered Mr. Adister's having said that military training was good for all gentlemen.

'I could join the French Foreign Legion,' he thought.

Adiante was as beautiful by day as by night. He looked. The riddle of her was more burdensome in the daylight.

He sighed, and on another surging of his admiration launched the resolve that he would serve her blindly, without one question. How, when, where, and the means and the aim, he did not think of. There was she, and here was he, and heaven and a great heart would show the way.

Adiante at eighteen, the full length of her, fresh in her love of Philip, was not the same person to him, she had not the same secret; she was beautiful differently. By right he should have loved the portrait best: but he had not seen it first; he had already lived through a life of emotions with the miniature, and could besides clasp the frame; and moreover he fondled an absurd notion that the miniature would be entrusted to him for a time, and was almost a possession. The pain of the thought of relinquishing it was the origin of this foolishness. And again, if it be fair to prove him so deeply, true to his brother though he was (admiration of a woman does thus influence the tides of our blood to render the noblest of us guilty of some unconscious wavering of our loyalty), Patrick dedicated the full-length of Adiante to Philip, and reserved the other, her face and neck, for himself.

Obediently to Mr. Adister's order, the portrait had been taken from one of his private rooms and placed in the armoury, the veil covering the canvas of late removed. Guns and spears and swords overhead and about, the youthful figure of Adiante was ominously encompassed. Caroline stood with Patrick before the portrait of her cousin; she expected him to show a sign of appreciation. He asked her to tell him the Church whose forms of faith the princess had embraced. She answered that it was the Greek Church. 'The Greek,' said he, gazing harder at the portrait. Presently she said: 'It was a perfect likeness.' She named the famous artist who had painted it. Patrick's 'Ah' was unsatisfactory.

'We,' said she, 'think it a living image of her as she was then.'

He would not be instigated to speak.

'You do not admire it, Mr. O'Donnell?' she cried.

'Oh, but I do. That's how she looked when she was drawing on her gloves with good will to go out to meet him. You can't see her there and not be sure she had a heart. She part smiles; she keeps her mouth shut, but there's the dimple, and it means a thought, like a bubble bursting up from the heart in her breast. She's tall. She carries herself like a great French lady, and nothing beats that. It's the same colour, dark eyebrows and fair hair. And not thinking of her pride. She thinks of her walk, and the end of it, where he's waiting. The eyes are not the same.'

'The same?' said Caroline.

'As this.' He tapped on the left side. She did not understand it at all.

'The bit of work done in Vienna,' said he.

She blushed. 'Do you admire that so much?'

'I do.'

'We consider it not to be compared to this.'

'Perhaps not. I like it better.'

'But why do you like that better?' said Caroline, deeming it his wilfulness.

Patrick put out a finger. 'The eyes there don't seem to say, "I'm yours to make a hero of you." But look,' he drew forth from under his waistcoat the miniature, 'what don't they say here! It's a bright day for the Austrian capital that has her by the river Danube. Yours has a landscape; I've made acquaintance with the country, I caught the print of it on my ride yesterday; and those are your mountains. But mine has her all to herself while she's thinking undisturbed in her boudoir. I have her and her thoughts; that's next to her soul. I've an idea it ought to be given to Philip.' He craned his head round to woo some shadow of assent to the daring suggestion. 'Just to break the shock 'twill be to my brother, Miss Adister. If I could hand him this, and say, "Keep it, for you'll get nothing more of her; and that's worth a kingdom."'

Caroline faltered: 'Your brother does not know?'

'Pity him. His blow 's to come. He can't or he 'd have spoken of it to me. I was with him a couple of hours and he never mentioned a word of it, nor did Captain Con. We talked of Ireland,

and the service, and some French cousins we have.'

'Ladies?' Caroline inquired by instinct.

'And charming,' said Patrick, 'real dear girls. Philip might have one, if he would, and half my property, to make it right with her parents. There'd be little use in proposing it. He was dead struck when the shaft struck him. That's love! So I determined the night after I'd shaken his hand I'd be off to Earlsfont and try my hardest for him. It's hopeless now. Only he might have the miniature for his bride. I can tell him a trifle to help him over his agony. She would have had him, she would, Miss Adister, if she hadn't feared he'd be talked of as Captain Con has been—about the neighbourhood, I mean, because he,' Patrick added hurriedly, 'he married an heiress and sank his ambition for distinction like a man who has finished his dinner. I'm certain she would. I have it on authority.'

'What authority?' said Caroline coldly.

'Her own old nurse.'

'Jenny Williams?'

'The one! I had it from her. And how she loves her darling Miss Adiante! She won't hear of "princess." She hates that marriage. She was all for my brother Philip. She calls him "Our handsome lieutenant." She'll keep the poor fellow a subaltern all his life.'

'You went to Jenny's inn?'

'The Earlsfont Arms, I went to. And Mrs. Jenny at the door, watching the rain. Destiny directed me. She caught the likeness to Philip on a lift of her eye, and very soon we sat conversing like old friends. We were soon playing at old cronies over past times. I saw the way to bring her out, so I set to work, and she was up in defence of her darling, ready to tell me anything to get me to think well of her. And that was the main reason, she said, why Miss Adiante broke with him and went abroad her dear child wouldn't have Mr. Philip abused for fortune-hunting. As for the religion, they could each have practised their own: her father would have consented to the fact, when it came on him in that undeniable shape of two made one. She says, Miss Adiante has a mighty soul; she has brave ideas. Miss Deenly, she calls her. Ay, and so has Philip: though the worst is, they're likely to drive him out of the army into politics and Parliament; and an Irishman there is a barrow trolling a load of grievances. Ah, but she would have kept him straight. Not a soldier alive knows the use of cavalry better than my brother. He wanted just that English wife to steady him and pour drops of universal fire into him; to keep him face to face with the world, I mean; letting him be true to his country in a fair degree, but not an old rainpipe and spout. She would have held him to his profession. And, Oh dear! She's a friend worth having, lost to Ireland. I see what she could have done there. Something bigger than an island, too, has to be served in our days: that is, if we don't forget our duty at home. Poor Paddy, and his pig, and his bit of earth! If you knew what we feel for him! I'm a landlord, but I'm one with my people about evictions. We Irish take strong root. And honest rent paid over to absentees, through an agent, if you think of it, seems like flinging the money that's the sweat of the brow into a stone conduit to roll away to a giant maw hungry as the sea. It's the bleeding to death of our land! Transactions from hand to hand of warm human flesh-nothing else will do: I mean, for men of our blood. Ah!

she would have kept my brother temperate in his notions and his plans. And why absentees, Miss Adister? Because we've no centre of home life: the core has been taken out of us; our country has no hearth-fire. I'm for union; only there should be justice, and a little knowledge to make allowance for the natural cravings of a different kind of people. Well, then, and I suppose that inter-marriages are good for both. But here comes a man, the boldest and handsomest of his race, and he offers himself to the handsomest and sweetest of yours, and she leans to him, and the family won't have him. For he's an Irishman and a Catholic. Who is it then opposed the proper union of the two islands? Not Philip. He did his best; and if he does worse now he's not entirely to blame. The misfortune is, that when he learns the total loss of her on that rock-promontory, he'll be dashing himself upon rocks sure to shiver him. There's my fear. If I might take him this...?' Patrick pleaded with the miniature raised like the figure of his interrogation.

Caroline's inward smile threw a soft light of humour over her features at the simple cunning of his wind-up to the lecture on his country's case, which led her to perceive a similar cunning simplicity in his identification of it with Philip's. It startled her to surprise, for the reason that she'd been reviewing his freakish hops from Philip to Ireland and to Adiante, and wondering in a different kind of surprise, how and by what profitless ingenuity he contrived to weave them together. Nor was she unmoved, notwithstanding her fancied perception of his Jesuitry: his look and his voice were persuasive; his love of his brother was deep; his change of sentiment toward Adiante after the tale told him by her old nurse Jenny, stood for proof of a generous manliness.

Before she had replied, her uncle entered the armoury, and Patrick was pleading still, and she felt herself to be a piece of damask, a very fiery dye.

To disentangle herself, she said on an impulse, desperately

'Mr. O'Donnell begs to have the miniature for his brother.'

Patrick swung instantly to Mr. Adister. 'I presumed to ask for it, sir, to carry it to Philip. He is ignorant about the princess as yet; he would like to have a bit of the wreck. I shan't be a pleasant messenger to him. I should be glad to take him something. It could be returned after a time. She was a great deal to Philip—three parts of his life. He has nothing of her to call his own.'

'That!' said Mr. Adister. He turned to the virgin Adiante, sat down and shut his eyes, fetching a breath. He looked vacantly at Patrick.

'When you find a man purely destructive, you think him a devil, don't you?' he said.

'A good first cousin to one,' Patrick replied, watchful for a hint to seize the connection.

'If you think of hunting to-day, we have not many minutes to spare before we mount. The meet is at eleven, five miles distant. Go and choose your horse. Caroline will drive there.'

Patrick consulted her on a glance for counsel. 'I shall be glad to join you, sir, for to-morrow I must be off to my brother.'

'Take it,' Mr. Adister waved his hand hastily. He gazed at his idol of untouched eighteen. 'Keep it safe,' he said, discarding the sight of the princess. 'Old houses are doomed to burnings, and a devil in the family may bring us to ashes. And some day...!' he could not continue his thought upon what he might be destined to wish for, and ran it on to, 'Some day I shall be happy to welcome your brother, when it pleases him to visit me.'

Patrick bowed, oppressed by the mighty gift. 'I haven't the word to thank you with, sir.'

Mr. Adister did not wait for it.

'I owe this to you, Miss Adister,' said Patrick.

Her voice shook: 'My uncle loves those who loved her.'

He could see she was trembling. When he was alone his ardour of gratefulness enabled him to see into her uncle's breast: the inflexible frigidity; lasting regrets and remorse; the compassion for Philip in kinship of grief and loss; the angry dignity; the stately generosity.

He saw too, for he was clear-eyed when his feelings were not over-active, the narrow pedestal whereon the stiff figure of a man of iron pride must accommodate itself to stand in despite of tempests without and within; and how the statue rocks there, how much more pitiably than the common sons of earth who have the broad common field to fall down on and our good mother's milk to set them on their legs again.

CHAPTER VIII. CAPTAIN CON AND MRS. ADISTER O'DONNELL

Riding homeward from the hunt at the leisurely trot of men who have steamed their mounts pretty well, Mr. Adister questioned Patrick familiarly about his family, and his estate, and his brother's prospects in the army, and whither he intended first to direct his travels: questions which Patrick understood to be kindly put for the sake of promoting conversation with a companion of unripe age by a gentleman who had wholesomely excited his blood to run. They were answered, except the last one. Patrick had no immediate destination in view.

'Leave Europe behind you,' said Mr. Adister warming, to advise him, and checking the trot of his horse. 'Try South America.' The lordly gentleman plotted out a scheme of colonisation and conquest in that region with the coolness of a practised freebooter. 'No young man is worth a job,' he said, 'who does not mean to be a leader, and as leader to have dominion. Here we are fettered by ancestry and antecedents. Had I to recommence without those encumbrances, I would try my fortune yonder. I stood condemned to waste my youth in idle parades, and hunting the bear and buffalo. The estate you have inherited is not binding on you. You can realise it, and begin by taking over two or three hundred picked Irish and English—have both races capable of handling spade and musket; purchasing some thousands of acres to establish a legal footing there.

'You increase your colony from the mother country in the ratio of your prosperity, until your power is respected, and there is a necessity for the extension of your territory. When you are feared you will be on your mettle. They will favour you with provocation. I should not doubt the result, supposing myself to have under my sole command a trained body of men of English blood—and Irish.'

'Owners of the soil,' rejoined Patrick, much marvelling.

'Undoubtedly, owners of the soil, but owing you service.'

'They fight sir'

'It is hardly to be specified in the calculation, knowing them. Soldiery who have served their term, particularly old artillerymen, would be my choice: young fellows and boys among them. Women would have to be taken. Half-breeds are the ruin of colonists. Our men are born for conquest. We were conquerors here, and it is want of action and going physically forward that makes us a rusty people. There are—Mr. Adister's intonation told of his proposing a wretched alternative,—'the Pacific Islands, but they will soon be snapped up by the European and North American Governments, and a single one of them does not offer space. It would require money and a navy.' He mused. 'South America is the quarter I should decide for, as a young man. You are a judge of horses; you ride well; you would have splendid pastures over there; you might raise a famous breed. The air is fine; it would suit our English stock. We are on ground, Mr. O'Donnell, which my forefathers contested sharply and did not yield.'

'The owners of the soil had to do that,' said Patrick. 'I can show the same in my country, with a difference.'

'Considerably to your benefit.'

'Everything has been crushed there barring the contrary opinion.'

'I could expect such a remark from a rebel.'

'I'm only interpreting the people, sir.'

'Jump out of that tinder-box as soon as you can.'

'When I was in South America, it astonished me that no Englishman had cast an eye on so inviting a land. Australia is not comparable with it. And where colonisations have begun without system, and without hard fighting to teach the settlers to value good leadership and respect their chiefs, they tumble into Republics.'

Patrick would have liked to fling a word in about the Englishman's cast of his eye upon inviting lands, but the trot was resumed, the lord of Earlsfont having delivered his mind, and a minute made it happily too late for the sarcastic bolt. Glad that his tongue had been kept from wagging, he trotted along beside his host in the dusky evening over the once contested land where the gentleman's forefathers had done their deeds and firmly fixed their descendants. A remainder of dull red fire prolonged the half-day above the mountain strongholds of the former owners of the soil, upon which prince and bard and priest, and grappling natives never wanting for fierceness, roared to-arms in the beacon-flames from ridge to peak: and down they poured, and back they were pushed by the inveterate coloniser—stationing at threatened points his old 'artillerymen' of those days and so it ends, that bard and priest and prince; holy poetry, and divine prescription, and a righteous holding; are as naught against him. They go, like yonder embers of the winter sunset before advancing night: and to morrow the beacon-heaps are ashes, the conqueror's foot stamps on them, the wind scatters them; strangest of all, you hear victorious lawlessness appealing solemnly to God the law.

Patrick was too young to philosophise upon his ideas; or else the series of pictures projected by the troops of sensations running through him were not of a solidity to support any structure of philosophy. He reverted, though rather in name than in spirit, to the abstractions, justice, consistency, right. They were too hard to think of, so he abandoned the puzzle of fitting them to men's acts and their consciences, and he put them aside as mere titles employed for the uses of a police and a tribunal to lend an appearance of legitimacy to the decrees of them that have got the upper hand. An insurrectionary rising of his breast on behalf of his country was the consequence. He kept it down by turning the whole hubbub within him to the practical contemplation of a visionary South America as the region for him and a fighting tenantry. With a woman, to crown her queen there, the prospect was fair. But where dwelt the woman possessing majesty suitable to such a dream in her heart or her head? The best he had known in Ireland and in France, preferred the charms of society to bold adventure.

All the same, thought he, it's queer counsel, that we should set to work by buying a bit of land to win a clean footing to rob our neighbours: and his brains took another shot at Mr. Adister, this time without penetrating. He could very well have seen the matter he disliked in a man that he disliked; but the father of Adiante had touched him with the gift of the miniature.

Patrick was not asked to postpone his departure from Earlsfont, nor was he invited to come again. Mr. Adister drove him to the station in the early morning, and gave him a single nod from the phaeton-box for a good-bye. Had not Caroline assured him at the leave-taking between them that he had done her uncle great good by his visit, the blank of the usual ceremonial phrases would have caused him to fancy himself an intruder courteously dismissed, never more to enter the grand old Hall. He was further comforted by hearing the stationmaster's exclamation of astonishment and pleasure at the sight of the squire 'in his place' handling the reins, which had not been witnessed for many a day and so it appeared that the recent guest had been exceptionally complimented. 'But why not a warm word, instead of turning me off to decipher a bit of Egyptian on baked brick,' he thought, incurably Celtic as he was.

From the moment when he beheld Mr. Adister's phaeton mounting a hill that took the first leap for the Cambrian highlands, up to his arrival in London, scarcely one of his 'ideas' darted out before Patrick, as they were in the habit of doing, like the enchanted hares of fairyland, tempting him to pursue, and changing into the form of woman ever, at some turn of the chase. For as he had travelled down to Earlsfont in the state of ignorance and hopefulness, bearing the liquid brains of that young condition, so did his acquisition of a particular fact destructive of hope solidify them about it as he travelled back: in other words, they were digesting what they had taken in. Imagination would not have stirred for a thousand fleeting hares: and principally, it may be, because he was conscious that no form of woman would anywhere come of them. Woman was married; she had the ring on her finger! He could at his option look on her in the miniature, he could think of her as being in the city where she had been painted; but he could not conjure her out of space; she was nowhere in the ambient air. Secretly she was a feeling that lay half slumbering very deep down within him, and he kept the secret, choosing to be poor rather than call her forth. He was in truth digesting with difficulty, as must be the case when it is allotted to the brains to absorb what the soul abhors.

'Poor old Philip!' was his perpetual refrain. 'Philip, the girl you loved is married; and here's her portrait taken in her last blush; and the man who has her hasn't a share in that!' Thus, throwing in the ghost of a sigh for sympathy, it seemed to Patrick that the intelligence would have to be communicated. Bang is better, thought he, for bad news than snapping fire and feinting, when you're bound half to kill a fellow, and a manly fellow.

Determined that bang it should be, he hurried from the terminus to Philip's hotel, where he had left him, and was thence despatched to the house of Captain Con O'Donnell, where he created a joyful confusion, slightly dashed with rigour on the part of the regnant lady; which is not to be wondered at, considering that both the gentlemen attending her, Philip and her husband, quitted her table with shouts at the announcement of his name, and her husband hauled him in unwashed before her, crying that the lost was found, the errant returned, the Prodigal Pat recovered by his kinsman! and she had to submit to the introduction of the disturber: and a bedchamber had to be thought of for the unexpected guest, and the dinner to be delayed in middle course, and her husband corrected between the discussions concerning the bedchamber, and either the guest permitted to appear at her table in sooty day-garb, or else a great gap commanded in the service of her dishes, vexatious extreme for a lady composed of orderliness. She acknowledged Patrick's profound salute and his excuses with just so many degrees in the inclining of her head as the polite deem a duty to themselves when the ruffling world has disarranged them.

'Con!' she called to her chattering husband, 'we are in England, if you please.'

'To be sure, madam,' said the captain, 'and so 's Patrick, thanks to the stars. We fancied him gone, kidnapped, burned, made a meal of and swallowed up, under the earth or the water; for he forgot to give us his address in town; he stood before us for an hour or so, and then the fellow vanished. We've waited for him gaping. With your permission I'll venture an opinion that he'll go and dabble his hands and sit with us as he is, for the once, as it happens.'

'Let it be so,' she rejoined, not pacified beneath her dignity. She named the bedchamber to a footman.

'And I'll accompany the boy to hurry him on,' said the captain, hurrying Patrick on as he spoke, till he had him out of the dining-room, when he whispered: 'Out with your key, and if we can scramble you into your evening-suit quick we shall heal the breach in the dinner. You dip your hands and face, I'll have out the dress. You've the right style for her, my boy: and mind, she is an excellent good woman, worthy of all respect: but formality's the flattery she likes: a good bow and short speech. Here we are, and the room's lighted. Off to the basin, give me the key; and here's hot water in tripping Mary's hands. The portmanteau opens easy. Quick! the door's shut on rosy Mary. The race is for domestic peace, my boy. I sacrifice everything I can for it, in decency. 'Tis the secret of my happiness.'

Patrick's transformation was rapid enough to satisfy the impatient captain, who said: 'You'll tell her you couldn't sit down in her presence undressed. I married her at forty, you know, when a woman has reached her perfect development, and leans a trifle more to ceremonies than to substance. And where have you been the while?'

'I'll tell you by and by,' said Patrick.

'Tell me now, and don't be smirking at the glass; your necktie's as neat as a lady's company-smile, equal at both ends, and warranted not to relax before the evening 's over. And mind you don't set me off talking over-much downstairs. I talk in her presence like the usher of the Court to the judge. 'Tis the secret of my happiness.'

'Where are those rascally dress-boots of mine?' cried Patrick.

Captain Con pitched the contents of the portmanteau right and left. 'Never mind the boots, my boy. Your legs will be under the table during dinner, and we'll institute a rummage up here between that and the procession to the drawing-room, where you'll be examined head to foot, devil a doubt of it. But say, where have you been? She'll be asking, and we're in a mess already, and may as well have a place to name to her, somewhere, to excuse the gash you've made in her dinner. Here they are, both of 'm, rolled in a dirty shirt!'

Patrick seized the boots and tugged them on, saying 'Earlsfont, then.'

'You've been visiting Earlsfont? Whack! but that's the saving of us! Talk to her of her brother he sends her his love. Talk to her of the ancestral hall—it stands as it was on the day of its foundation. Just wait about five minutes to let her punish us, before you out with it. 'Twill come best from you. What did you go down there for? But don't stand answering questions; come along. Don't heed her countenance at the going in: we've got the talisman. As to the dressing, it's a perfect trick of harlequinade, and she'll own it after a dose of Earlsfont. And, by the way, she's not Mrs. Con, remember; she's Mrs. Adister O'Donnell: and that's best rolled out to Mistress. She's a worthy woman, but she was married at forty, and I had to take her shaped as she was, for moulding her at all was out of the question, and the soft parts of me had to be the sufferers, to effect a conjunction, for where one won't and can't, poor t' other must, or the union's a mockery. She was cast in bronze at her birth, if she wasn't cut in bog-root. Anyhow, you'll study her. Consider her for my sake. Madam, it should be—madam, call her, addressing her, madam. She hasn't a taste for jokes, and she chastises absurdities, and England's the foremost country of the globe, indirect communication with heaven, and only to be connected with such a country by the tail of it is a special distinction and a comfort for us; we're that part of the kite!—but, Patrick, she's a charitable soul; she's a virtuous woman and an affectionate wife, and doesn't frown to see me turn off to my place of worship while she drum-majors it away to her own; she entertains Father Boyle heartily, like the good woman she is to good men; and unfortunate females too have a friend in her, a real friend—that they have; and that 's a wonder in a woman chaste as ice. I do respect her; and I'd like to see the man to favour me with an opportunity of proving it on him! So you'll not forget, my boy; and prepare for a cold bath the first five minutes. Out with Earlsfont early after that. All these things are trifles to an unmarried man. I have to attend to 'm, I have to be politic and give her elbow-room for her natural angles. 'Tis the secret of my happiness.'

Priming his kinsman thus up to the door of the diningroom, Captain Con thrust him in.

Mistress Adister O'Donnell's head rounded as by slow attraction to the clock. Her disciplined husband signified an equal mixture of contrition and astonishment at the passing of time. He fell to work upon his plate in obedience to the immediate policy dictated to him.

The unbending English lady contrasted with her husband so signally that the oddly united couple appeared yoked in a common harness for a perpetual display of the opposition of the races. She resembled her brother, the lord of Earlsfont, in her remarkable height and her calm air of authority and self-sustainment. From beneath a head-dress built of white curls and costly lace, half enclosing her high narrow forehead, a pale, thin, straight bridge of nose descended prominently over her sunken cheeks to thin locked lips. Her aspect suggested the repose of a winter landscape, enjoyable in pictures, or on skates, otherwise nipping.... Mental directness, of no greater breadth than her principal feature, was the character it expressed; and candour of spirit shone through the transparency she was, if that mild taper could be said to shine in proof of a vitality rarely notified to the outer world by the opening of her mouth; chiefly then, though not malevolently to command: as the portal of some snow-bound monastery opens to the outcast, bidding it be known that the light across the wolds was not deceptive and a glimmer of light subsists among the silent within. The life sufficed to her. She was like a marble effigy seated upright, requiring but to be laid at her length for transport to the cover of the tomb.

Now Captain Con was by nature ruddy as an Indian summer flushed in all its leaves. The corners of his face had everywhere a frank ambush, or child's hiding-place, for languages and laughter. He could worm with a smile quite his own the humour out of men possessing any; and even under rigorous law, and it could not be disputed that there was rigour in the beneficent laws imposed upon him by his wife, his genius for humour and passion for sly independence came up and curled away like the smoke of the illicit still, wherein the fanciful discern fine sprites indulging in luxurious grimaces at a government long-nosed to no purpose. Perhaps, as Patrick said of him to Caroline Adister, he was a bard without a theme. He certainly was a man of speech, and the having fearfully to contain himself for the greater number of the hours of the day, for the preservation of the domestic felicity he had learnt to value, fathered the sentiment of revolt in his bosom.

By this time, long after five minutes had elapsed, the frost presiding at the table was fast withering Captain Con; and he was irritable to hear why Patrick had gone off to Earlsfont, and what he had done there, and the adventures he had tasted on the road; anything for warmth. His efforts to fish the word out of Patrick produced deeper crevasses in the conversation, and he cried to himself: Hats and crape-bands! mightily struck by an idea that he and his cousins were a party of hired mourners over the meat they consumed. Patrick was endeavouring to spare his brother a mention of Earlsfont before they had private talk together. He answered neither to a dip of the hook nor to a pull.

'The desert where you 've come from 's good,' said the captain, sharply nodding.

Mrs. Adister O'Donnell ejaculated: 'Wine!' for a heavy comment upon one of his topics, and crushed it.

Philip saw that Patrick had no desire to spread, and did not trouble him.

'Good horses in the stable too,' said the captain.

Patrick addressed Mrs. Adister: 'I have hardly excused myself to you, madam.'

Her head was aloft in dumb apostrophe of wearifulness over another of her husband's topics.

'Do not excuse yourself at all,' she said.

The captain shivered. He overhauled his plotting soul publicly: 'Why don't you out with it yourself!' and it was wonderful why he had not done so, save that he was prone to petty conspiracy, and had thought reasonably that the revelation would be damp, gunpowder, coming from him. And for when he added: 'The boy's fresh from Earlsfont; he went down to look at the brav old house of the Adisters, and was nobly welcomed and entertained, and made a vast impression,' his wife sedately remarked to Patrick, 'You have seen my brother Edward.'

'And brings a message of his love to you, my dear,' the Captain bit his nail harder.

'You have a message for me?' she asked; and Patrick replied: 'The captain is giving a free translation. I was down there, and I took the liberty of calling on Mr. Adister, and I had a very kind reception. We hunted, we had a good day with the hounds. I think I remember hearing that you go there at Christmas, madam.'

'Our last Christmas at Earlsfont was a sad meeting for the family. My brother Edward is well?'

'I had the happiness to be told that I had been of a little service in cheering him.'

'I can believe it,' said Mrs. Adister, letting her eyes dwell on the young man; and he was moved by the silvery tremulousness of her voice.

She resumed: 'You have the art of dressing in a surprisingly short time.'

'There!' exclaimed Captain Con: for no man can hear the words which prove him a prophet without showing excitement. 'Didn't I say so? Patrick's a hero for love or war, my dear. He stood neat and trim from the silk socks to the sprig of necktie in six minutes by my watch. And that's witness to me that you may count on him for what the great Napoleon called two-o'clock-in-the-morning courage; not too common even in his immortal army:—when it's pitch black and frosty cold, and you're buried within in a dream of home, and the trumpet springs you to your legs in a trice, boots and trowsers, coat and sword-belt and shako, and one twirl to the whiskers, and away before a second snap of the fingers to where the great big bursting end of all things for you lies crouching like a Java-Tiger—a ferocious beast painted undertaker's colour—for a leap at you in particular out of the dark;—never waiting an instant to ask what's the matter and pretend you don't know. That's rare, Philip; that's bravery; Napoleon knew the thing; and Patrick has it; my hand's on the boy's back for that.'

The captain was permitted to discourse as he pleased: his wife was wholly given to the recent visitor to Earlsfont, whom she informed that Caroline was the youngest daughter of General Adister, her second brother, and an excellent maiden, her dear Edward's mainstay in his grief. At last she rose, and was escorted to the door by all present. But Captain Con rather shame-facedly explained to Patrick that it was a sham departure; they had to follow without a single spin to the claretjug: he closed the door merely to state his position; how at half-past ten he would be a free man, according to the convention, to which his wife honourably adhered, so he had to do likewise, as regarded his share of it. Thereupon he apologised to the brothers, bitterly regretting that, with good wine in the cellar, his could be no house for claret; and promising them they should sit in their shirts and stretch their legs, and toast the old country and open their hearts, no later than the minute pointing to the time for his deliverance.

Mrs. Adister accepted her husband's proffered arm unhesitatingly at the appointed stroke of the clock. She said: 'Yes,' in agreement with him, as if she had never heard him previously enunciate the formula, upon his pious vociferation that there should be no trifling with her hours of rest.

'You can find your way to my cabin,' he said to Philip over his shoulder, full of solicitude for the steps of the admirable lady now positively departing.

As soon as the brothers were alone, Philip laid his hand on Patrick, asking him, 'What does it mean?'

Patrick fired his cannon-shot: 'She's married!' Consulting his feelings immediately after, he hated himself for his bluntness.

Philip tossed his head. 'But why did you go down there?'

'I went,' said Patrick, 'well, I went.... I thought you looked wretched, and I went with an idea of learning where she was, and seeing if I couldn't do something. It's too late now; all's over.'

'My dear boy, I've worse than that to think of.'

'You don't mind it?'

'That's old news, Patrick.'

'You don't care for her any more, Philip?'

'You wouldn't have me caring for a married woman?'

'She has a perfect beast for a husband.'
'I'm sorry she didn't make a better choice.'
'He's a prince.'
'So I hear.'
'Ah! And what worse, Philip, can you be having to think of?'
'Affairs,' Philip replied, and made his way to the cabin of Captain Con, followed in wonderment by Patrick, who would hardly have been his dupe to suppose him indifferent and his love of Adiante dead, had not the thought flashed on him a prospect of retaining the miniature for his own, or for long in his custody.

CHAPTER IX. THE CAPTAIN'S CABIN

Patrick left his brother at the second flight of stairs to run and fling on a shooting-jacket, into which he stuffed his treasure, after one peep that eclipsed his little dream of being allowed to keep it; and so he saw through Philip.

The captain's cabin was the crown of his house-top, a builder's addition to the roof, where the detestable deeds he revelled in, calling them liberty, could be practised, according to the convention, and no one save rosy Mary, in her sense of smell, when she came upon her morning business to clean and sweep, be any the wiser of them, because, as it is known to the whole world, smoke ascends, and he was up among the chimneys. Here, he would say to his friends and fellow-sinners, you can unfold, unbosom, explode, do all you like, except caper, and there's a small square of lead between the tiles outside for that, if the spirit of the jig comes upon you with violence, as I have had it on me, and eased myself mightily there, to my own music; and the capital of the British Empire below me. Here we take our indemnity for subjection to the tyrannical female ear, and talk like copious rivers meandering at their own sweet will. Here we roll like dogs in carrion, and no one to sniff at our coats. Here we sing treason, here we flout reason, night is out season at half-past ten.

This introductory ode to Freedom was his throwing off of steam, the foretaste of what he contained. He rejoined his cousins, chirping variations on it, and attired in a green silken suit of airy Ottoman volume, full of incitement to the legs and arms to swing and set him up for a Sultan. 'Now Phil, now Pat,' he cried, after tenderly pulling the door to and making sure it was shut, 'any tale you've a mind for—infamous and audacious! You're licensed by the gods up here, and may laugh at them too, and their mothers and grandmothers, if the fit seizes ye, and the heartier it is the greater the exemption. We're pots that knock the lid and must pour out or boil over and destroy the furniture. My praties are ready for peelin', if ever they were in this world! Chuck wigs from sconces, and off with your buckram. Decency's a dirty petticoat in the Garden of Innocence. Naked we stand, boys! we're not afraid of nature. You're in the annexe of Erin, Pat, and devil a constable at the keyhole; no rats; I'll say that for the Government, though it's a despotism with an iron bridle on the tongue outside to a foot of the door. Arctic to freeze the boldest bud of liberty! I'd like a French chanson from ye, Pat, to put us in tune, with a right revolutionary hurling chorus, that pitches Kings' heads into the basket like autumn apples. Or one of your hymns in Gaelic sung ferociously to sound as horrid to the Saxon, the wretch. His reign's not for ever; he can't enter here. You're in the stronghold defying him. And now cigars, boys, pipes; there are the boxes, there are the bowls. I can't smoke till I have done steaming. I'll sit awhile silently for the operation. Christendom hasn't such a man as your cousin Con for feeling himself a pig-possessed all the blessed day, acting the part of somebody else, till it takes me a quarter of an hour of my enfranchisement and restoration of my natural man to know myself again. For the moment, I'm froth, scum, horrid boiling hissing dew of the agony of transformation; I am; I'm that pig disgorging the spirit of wickedness from his poor stomach.'

The captain drooped to represent the state of the self-relieving victim of the evil one; but fearful lest either of his cousins should usurp the chair and thwart his chance of delivering himself, he rattled away sympathetically with his posture in melancholy: 'Ay, we're poor creatures; pigs and prophets, princes and people, victors and vanquished, we're waves of the sea, rolling over and over, and calling it life! There's no life save the eternal. Father Boyle's got the truth. Flesh is less than grass, my sons; 'tis the shadow that crosses the grass. I love the grass. I could sit and watch grassblades for hours. I love an old turf mound, where the grey grass nods and seems to know the wind and have a whisper with it, of ancient times maybe and most like; about the big chief lying underneath in the last must of his bones that a breath of air would scatter. They just keep their skeleton shape as they are; for the turf mound protects them from troubles: 'tis the nurse to that delicate old infant!—Waves of the sea, did I say? We're wash in a hog-trough for Father Saturn to devour; big chief and suckling babe, we all go into it, calling it life! And what hope have we of reading the mystery? All we can see is the straining of the old fellow's hams to push his old snout deeper into the gobble, and the ridiculous curl of a tail totally devoid of expression! You'll observe that gluttons have no feature; they're jaws and hindquarters; which is the beginning and end of 'm; and so you may say to Time for his dealing with us: so let it be a lesson to you not to bother your wits, but leave the puzzle to the priest. He understands it, and why? because he was told. There's harmony in his elocution, and there's none in the modern drivel about where we're going and what we came out of. No wonder they call it an age of despair, when you see the big wigs filing up and down the thoroughfares with a great advertisement board on their shoulders, proclaiming no information to the multitude, but a blank note of interrogation addressed to Providence, as if an answer from above would be vouchsafed to their impudence! They haven't the first principles of good manners. And some of 'm in a rage bawl the answer for themselves. Hear that! No, Phil; No, Pat, no: devotion's good policy.— You're not drinking! Are you both of ye asleep? why do ye leave me to drone away like this, when it's conversation I want, as in the days of our first parents, before the fig-leaf?—and you might have that for scroll and figure on the social banner of the hypocritical Saxon, who's a gormandising animal behind his decency, and nearer to the Arch-devourer Time than anything I can imagine: except that with a little exertion you can elude him. The whisky you've got between you's virgin of the excise. I'll pay double for freepeaty any day. Or are you for claret, my lads? No? I'm fortified up here to stand a siege in my old round tower, like the son of Eremon that I am. Lavra Con! Con speaks at last! I don't ask you, Pat, whether you remember Maen, who was born dumb, and had for his tutors Ferkelne the bard and Crafting the harper, at pleasant Dinree: he was grandson of Leary Lore who was basely murdered by his brother Cova, and Cova spared the dumb boy, thinking a man without a tongue harmless, as fools do: being one of their savings-bank tricks, to be repaid them, their heirs, executors, administrators, and assigns at compound interest, have no fear. So one day Maen had an insult put on him; and 'twas this for certain: a ruffian fellow of the Court swore he couldn't mention the name of his father; and in a thundering fury Maen burst his tongue-tie, and the Court shouted Lavra Maen: and he had to go into exile, where he married in the middle of delicious love-adventures the beautiful Moira through the cunning of Craftine the harper. There's been no harper in my instance but plenty of ruffians to swear I'm too comfortable to think of my country.' The captain holloaed. 'Do they hear that? Lord! but wouldn't our old Celtic fill the world with poetry if only we were a free people to give our minds to 't, instead of to the itch on our backs from the Saxon horsehair shirt we're forced to wear. For, Pat, as you know, we're a loving people, we're a loyal people, we burn to be enthusiastic, but when our skins are eternally irritated, how can we sing? In a freer Erin I'd be the bard of the land, never doubt it. What am I here but a discontented idle lout crooning over the empty glories of our isle of Saints! You feel them, Pat. Phil's all for his British army, his capabilities of British light cavalry. Write me the history of the Enniskillens. I'll read it. Aha, my boy, when they 're off at the charge! And you'll oblige me with the tale of Fontenoy. Why, Phil has an opportunity stretching forth a hand to him now more than halfway that comes to a young Irishman but once in a century: backed by the entire body of the priesthood of Ireland too! and if only he was a quarter as full of the old country as you and I, his hair would stand up in fire for the splendid gallop at our head that's proposed to him. His country's gathered up like a crested billow to roll him into Parliament; and I say, let him be there, he 's the very man to hurl his gauntlet, and tell 'm, Parliament, so long as you are parliamentary, which means the speaking of our minds, but if you won't have it, then-and it 's on your heads before Europe and the two Americas. We're dying like a nun that 'd be out of her cloister, we're panting like the wife who hears of her husband coming home to her from the field of honour, for that young man. And there he is; or there he seems to be; but he's dead: and the fisherman off the west coast after dreaming of a magical haul, gets more fish than disappointment in comparison with us when we cast the net for Philip. Bring tears of vexation at the emptiness we pull back for our pains. Oh, Phil! and to think of your youth! We had you then. At least we had your heart. And we should have had the length and strength of you, only for a woman fatal to us as the daughter of Rhys ap Tudor, the beautiful Nesta:—and beautiful she was to match the mother of the curses trooping over to Ireland under Strongbow, that I'll grant you. But she reined you in when you were a real warhorse ramping and snorting flame from your nostrils, challenging any other to a race for Ireland; ay, a Cuchullin you were, Philip, Culann's chain-bound: but she unmanned you. She soaked the woman into you and squeezed the hero out of you. All for Adiante! or a country left to slavery! that's the tale. And what are you now? A paltry captain of hussars on the General's staff! One O'Donnell in a thousand! And what is she?—you needn't frown, Phil; I'm her relative by marriage, and she 's a lady. More than that, she shot a dart or two into my breast in those days, she did, I'll own it: I had the catch of the breath that warns us of convulsions. She was the morning star for beauty, between night and day, and the best colour of both. Welshmen and Irishmen and Englishmen tumbled into the pit, which seeing her was, and there we jostled for a glimpse quite companionably; we were too hungry for quarrelling; and to say, I was one of 'm, is a title to subsequent friendship. True; only mark me, Philip, and you, Patrick: they say she has married a prince, and I say no; she's took to herself a husband in her cradle; she's married ambition. I tell you, and this prince of hers is only a step she has taken, and if he chases her first mate from her bosom, he'll prove himself cleverer than she, and I dare him to the trial. For she's that fiery dragon, a beautiful woman with brains—which Helen of Troy hadn't, combustible as we know her to have been: but brains are bombshells in comparison with your old-fashioned pine-brands for kindling men and cities. Ambition's the husband of Adiante Adister, and all who come nigh her are steps to her aim. She never consulted her father about Prince Nikolas; she had begun her march and she didn't mean to be arrested. She simply announced her approaching union; and as she couldn't have a scion of one of the Royal House of Europe, she put her foot on Prince Nikolas. And he 's not to fancy he 's in for a peaceful existence; he's a stone in a sling, and probably mistaken the rocking that's to launch him through the air for a condition of remarkable ease, perfectly remarkable in its lullaby motion; ha! well, and I've not heard of ambition that didn't kill its votary: somehow it will; 'tis sure to. There she lies!'

The prophetic captain pointed at the spot. He then said: 'And now I'm for my pipe, and the blackest clay of the party, with your permission. I'll just go to the window to see if the stars are out overhead. They're my blessed guardian angels.'

There was a pause. Philip broke from a brown study to glance at his brother. Patrick made a queer face.

'Fun and good-fellowship to-night, Con,' said Philip, as the captain sadly reported no star visible.

'Have I ever flown a signal to the contrary?' retorted the captain.

'No politics, and I 'll thank you,' said Philip: 'none of your early recollections. Be jovial.'

'You should have seen me here the other night about a month ago; I smuggled up an old countrywoman of ours, with the connivance of rosy Mary,' said Captain Con, suffused in the merriest of grins. 'She sells apples at a stall at a corner of a street hard by, and I saw her sitting pulling at her old pipe in the cold October fog morning and evening for comfort, and was overwhelmed with compassion and fraternal sentiment; and so I invited her to be at the door of the house at half-past ten, just to have a roll with her in Irish mud, and mend her torn soul with a stitch or two of rejoicing. She told me stories; and one was pretty good, of a relative of hers, or somebody's—I should say, a century old, but she told it with a becoming air of appropriation that made it family history, for she's come down in the world, and this fellow had a stain of red upon him, and wanted cleaning; and, "What!" says the good father, "Mika! you did it in cold blood?" And says Mika, "Not I, your Riverence. I got myself into a passion 'fore I let loose." I believe she smoked this identical pipe. She acknowledged the merits of my whisky, as poets do hearing fine verses, never clapping hands, but with the expressiveness of grave absorption. That's the way to make good things a part of you. She was a treat. I got her out and off at midnight, rosy Mary sneaking her down, and the old girl quiet as a mouse for the fun's sake. The whole intrigue was exquisitely managed.'

'You run great risks,' Philip observed.

'I do,' said the captain.

He called on the brothers to admire the 'martial and fumial' decorations of his round tower, buzzing over the display of implements, while Patrick examined guns and Philip unsheathed swords. An ancient clay pipe from the bed of the Thames and one from the bed of the Boyne were laid side by side, and strange to relate, the Irish pipe and English immediately, by the mere fact of their being proximate, entered into rivalry; they all but leapt upon one another. The captain judicially decided the case against the English pipe, as a newer pipe of grosser manufacture, not so curious by any means.

'This,' Philip held up the reputed Irish pipe, and scanned as he twirled it on his thumb, 'This was dropped in Boyne Water by one of William's troopers. It is an Orange pipe. I take it to be of English make.'

'If I thought that, I'd stamp my heel on the humbug the neighbour minute,' said Captain Con. 'Where's the sign of English marks?'

'The pipes resemble one another,' said Philip, 'like tails of Shannon-bred retrievers.'

'Maybe they 're both Irish, then?' the captain caught at analogy to rescue his favourite from reproach.

'Both of them are Saxon.'

'Not a bit of it!'

'Look at the clay.'

'I look, and I tell you, Philip, it's of a piece with your lukewarmness for the country, or you wouldn't talk like that.'

'There is no record of pipe manufactories in Ireland at the period you name.'

'There is: and the jealousy of rulers caused them to be destroyed by decrees, if you want historical evidence.'

'Your opposition to the Saxon would rob him of his pipe, Con!'

'Let him go to the deuce with as many pipes as he can carry; but he shan't have this one.'

'Not a toss-up of difference is to be seen in the pair.'

'Use your eyes. The Irish bowl is broken, and the English has an inch longer stem!'

'O the Irish bowl is broken!' Philip sang.

'You've the heart of a renegade-foreigner not to see it!' cried the captain.

Patrick intervened saying: 'I suspect they're Dutch.'

'Well, and that 's possible.' Captain Con scrutinised them to calm his temper: 'there's a Dutchiness in the shape.'

He offered Philip the compromise of 'Dutch' rather plaintively, but it was not accepted, and the pipes would have mingled their fragments on the hearthstone if Patrick had not stayed his arm, saying: 'Don't hurt them.'

'And I won't,' the captain shook his hand gratefully.

'But will Philip O'Donnell tell me that Ireland should lie down with England on the terms of a traveller obliged to take a bedfellow? Come! He hasn't an answer. Put it to him, and you pose him. But he 'll not stir, though he admits the antagonism. And Ireland is asked to lie down with England on a couch blessed by the priest! Not she. Wipe out our grievances, and then we'll begin to talk of policy. Good Lord!—love? The love of Ireland for the conquering country will be the celebrated ceremony in the concluding chapter previous to the inauguration of the millennium. Thousands of us are in a starving state at home this winter, Patrick. And it's not the fault of England?—landlordism 's not? Who caused the ruin of all Ireland's industries? You might as well say that it's the fault of the poor beggar to go limping and hungry because his cruel master struck him a blow to cripple him. We don't want half and half doctoring, and it's too late in the day for half and half oratory. We want freedom, and we'll have it, and we won't leave it to the Saxon to think about giving it. And if your brother Philip won't accept this blazing fine offer, then I will, and you'll behold me in a new attitude. The fellow yawns! You don't know me yet, Philip. They tell us over here we ought to be satisfied. Fall upon our list of wrongs, and they set to work yawning. You can only move them by popping at them over hedges and roaring on platforms. They're incapable of understanding a complaint a yard beyond their noses. The Englishman has an island mind, and when he's out of it he's at sea.'

'Mad, you mean,' said Philip.

'I repeat my words, Captain Philip O'Donnell, late of the staff of the General commanding in Canada.'

'The Irishman too has an island mind, and when he's out of it he's at sea, and unable to manage his craft,' said Philip.

'You'll find more craft in him when he's buffeted than you reckoned on,' his cousin flung back. 'And if that isn't the speech of a traitor sold to the enemy, and now throwing off the mask, traitors never did mischief in Ireland! Why, what can you discover to admire in these people? Isn't their army such a combination of colours in the uniforms, with their yellow facings on red jackets, I never saw out of a doll-shop, and never saw there. And their Horse Guards, weedy to a man! fit for a doll-shop they are, by my faith! And their Foot Guards: Have ye met the fellows marching? with their feet turned out, flat as my laundress's irons, and the muscles of their calves depending on the joints to get 'm along, for elasticity never gave those bones of theirs a springing touch; and their bearskins heeling behind on their polls; like pot-house churls daring the dursn't to come on. Of course they can fight. Who said no? But they're not the only ones: and they'll miss their ranks before they can march like our Irish lads. The look of their men in line is for all the world to us what lack-lustre is to the eye. The drill they've had hasn't driven Hodge out of them, it has only stiffened the dolt; and dolt won't do any longer; the military machine requires intelligence in all ranks now. Ay, the time for the Celt is dawning: I see it, and I don't often spy a spark where there isn't soon a blaze. Solidity and stupidity have had their innings: a precious long innings it has been; and now they're shoved aside like clods of earth from the risin flower. Off with our shackles! We've only to determine it to be free, and we'll bloom again; and I'll be the first to speak the word and mount the colours. Follow me! Will ye join in the toast to the emblem of Erin—the shamrock, Phil and Pat?'

'Oh, certainly,' said Philip. 'What's that row going on?' Patrick also called attention to the singular noise in the room. 'I fancy the time for the Celt is not dawning, but setting,' said Philip, with a sharp smile; and Patrick wore an artful look.

A corner of the room was guilty of the incessant alarum. Captain Con gazed in that direction incredulously and with remonstrance. 'The tinkler it is!' he sighed. 'But it can't be midnight yet?' Watches were examined. Time stood at half-past the midnight. He groaned: 'I must go. I haven't heard the tinkler for months. It signifies she's cold in her bed. The thing called circulation's unknown to her save by the aid of outward application, and I 'm the warming pan, as legitimately I should be, I'm her husband and her Harvey in one. Goodbye to my hop and skip. I ought by rights to have been down beside her at midnight. She's the worthiest woman alive, and I don't shirk my duty. Be quiet!' he bellowed at the alarum; 'I 'm coming. Don't be in such a fright, my dear,' he admonished it as his wife, politely. 'Your hand'll take an hour to warm if you keep it out on the spring that sets the creature going.' He turned and informed his company: 'Her hand'll take an hour to warm. Dear! how she runs ahead: d' ye hear? That's the female tongue, and once off it won't stop. And this contrivance for fetching me from my tower to her bed was my own suggestion, in a fit of generosity! Ireland all over! I must hurry and wash my hair, for she can't bear a perfume to kill a stink; she carries her charitable heart that far. Good-night, I'll be thinking of ye while I'm warming her. Sit still, I can't wait; 'tis the secret of my happiness.' He fled. Patrick struck his knee on hearing the expected ballad-burden recur.

CHAPTER X. THE BROTHERS: 'Con has learnt one secret,' said Philip, quitting his chair.

Patrick went up to him, and, 'Give us a hug,' he said, and the hug was given.

They were of an equal height, tall young men, alert, nervously braced from head to foot, with the differences between soldier and civilian marked by the succintly military bearing of the elder brother, whose movements were precise and prompt, and whose frame was leopardlike in indolence. Beside him Patrick seemed cubbish, though beside another he would not have appeared so. His features were not so brilliantly regular, but were a fanciful sketch of the same design, showing a wider pattern of the long square head and the forehead, a wavering at the dip of the nose, livelier nostrils: the nostrils dilated and contracted, and were exceeding alive. His eyelids had to do with the look of his eyes, and were often seen cutting the ball. Philip's eyes were large on the pent of his brows, open, liquid, and quick with the fire in him. Eyes of that quality are the visible mind, animated both to speak it and to render it what comes within their scope. They were full, unshaded direct, the man himself, in action. Patrick's mouth had to be studied for an additional index to the character. To symbolise them, they were as a sword-blade lying beside book.

Men would have thought Patrick the slippery one of the two: women would have inclined to confide in him the more thoroughly; they bring feeling to the test, and do not so much read a print as read the imprinting on themselves; and the report that a certain one of us is true as steel, must be unanimous at a propitious hour to assure them completely that the steel is not two-edged in the fully formed nature of a man whom they have not tried. They are more at home with the unformed, which lends itself to feeling and imagination. Besides Patrick came nearer to them; he showed sensibility. They have it, and they deem it auspicious of goodness, or of the gentleness acceptable as an equivalent. Not the less was Philip the one to inspire the deeper and the wilder passion.

'So you've been down there?' said Philip. 'Tell us of your welcome. Never mind why you went: I think I see. You're the Patrick of fourteen, who tramped across Connaught for young Dermot to have a sight of you before he died, poor lad. How did Mr. Adister receive you?'

Patrick described the first interview.

Philip mused over it. 'Yes, those are some of his ideas: gentlemen are to excel in the knightly exercises. He used to fence excellently, and he was a good horseman. The Jesuit seminary would have been hard for him to swallow once. The house is a fine old house: lonely, I suppose.'

Patrick spoke of Caroline Adister and pursued his narrative. Philip was lost in thought. At the conclusion, relating to South America, he raised his head and said: 'Not so foolish as it struck you, Patrick. You and I might do that,—without the design upon the original owner of the soil! Irishmen are better out of Europe, unless they enter one of the Continental services.'

'What is it Con O'Donnell proposes to you?' Patrick asked him earnestly.

'To be a speaking trumpet in Parliament. And to put it first among the objections, I haven't an independence; not above two hundred a year.'

'I'll make it a thousand,' said Patrick, 'that is, if my people can pay.'

'Secondly, I don't want to give up my profession. Thirdly, fourthly, fifthly, once there, I should be boiling with the rest. I never could go half way. This idea of a commencement gives me a view of the finish. Would you care to try it?'

'If I'm no wiser after two or three years of the world I mean to make a better acquaintance with,' Patrick replied. 'Over there at home one catches the fever, you know. They have my feelings, and part of my judgement, and whether that's the weaker part I can't at present decide. My taste is for quiet farming and breeding.'

'Friendship, as far as possible; union, if the terms are fair,' said Philip. 'It's only the name of union now; supposing it a concession that is asked of them; say, sacrifice; it might be made for the sake of what our people would do to strengthen the nation. But they won't try to understand our people. Their laws, and their rules, their systems are forced on a race of an opposite temper, who would get on well enough, and thrive, if they were properly consulted. Ireland 's the sore place of England, and I'm sorry for it. We ought to be a solid square, with Europe in this pickle. So I say, sitting here. What should I be saying in Parliament?'

'Is Con at all likely, do you think, Philip?'

'He might: and become the burlesque Irishman of the House. There must be one, and the lot would be safe to fall on him.'

'Isn't he serious about it?'

'Quite, I fancy; and that will be the fun. A serious fellow talking nonsense with lively illustrations, is just the man for House of Commons clown. Your humorous rogue is not half so taking. Con would be the porpoise in a fish tank there, inscrutably busy on his errand and watched for his tumblings. Better I than he; and I should make a worse of it—at least for myself.'

'Wouldn't the secret of his happiness interfere?'

'If he has the secret inside his common sense. The bulk of it I suspect to be, that he enjoys his luxuries and is ashamed of his laziness; and so the secret pulls both ways. One day a fit of pride may have him, or one of his warm impulses, and if he's taken in the tide of it, I shall grieve for the secret.'

'You like his wife, Philip?'

'I respect her. They came together,—I suppose, because they were near together, like the two islands, in spite of the rolling waves between. I would not willingly see the union disturbed. He warms her, and she houses him. And he has to control the hot blood that does the warming, and she to moderate the severity of her principles, which are an essential part of the housing. Oh! shiver politics, Patrice. I wish I had been bred in France: a couple of years with your Pere Clement, and I could have met Irishmen and felt to them as an Irishman, whether they were disaffected or not. I wish I did. When I landed the other day, I thought myself passably cured, and could have said that rhetoric is the fire-water of our country, and claptrap the springboard to send us diving into it. I like my comrades-in-arms, I like the character of British officers, and the men too—I get on well with them. I declare to you, Patrice, I burn to live in brotherhood with them, not a rift of division at heart! I never show them that there is one. But our early training has us; it comes on us again; three or four days with Con have stirred me; I don't let him see it, but they always do: these tales of starvations and shootings, all the old work just as when I left, act on me like a smell of powder. I was dipped in "Ireland for the Irish"; and a contented Irishman scarcely seems my countryman.'

'I suppose it's like what I hear of as digesting with difficulty,' Patrick referred to the state described by his brother.

'And not the most agreeable of food,' Philip added.

'It would be the secret of our happiness to discover how to make the best of it, if we had to pay penance for the discovery by living in an Esquimaux shanty,' said Patrick.

'With a frozen fish of admirable principles for wife,' said Philip.

'Ah, you give me shudders!'

'And it's her guest who talks of her in that style! and I hope to be thought a gentleman!' Philip pulled himself up. 'We may be all in the wrong. The way to begin to think so, is to do them an injury and forget it. The sensation's not unpleasant when it's other than a question of good taste. But politics to bed, Patrice. My chief is right—soldiers have nothing to do with them. What are you fiddling at in your coat there?'

'Something for you, my dear Philip.' Patrick brought out the miniature. He held it for his brother to look. 'It was the only thing I could get. Mr. Adister sends it. The young lady, Miss Caroline, seconded me. They think more of the big portrait: I don't. And it's to be kept carefully, in case of the other one getting damaged. That's only fair.'

Philip drank in the face upon a swift shot of his eyes.

'Mr. Adister sends it?' His tone implied wonder at such a change in Adiante's father.

'And an invitation to you to visit him when you please.'

'That he might do,' said Philip: it was a lesser thing than to send her likeness to him.

Patrick could not help dropping his voice: 'Isn't it very like?' For answer the miniature had to be inspected closely.

Philip was a Spartan for keeping his feelings under.

'Yes,' he said, after an interval quick with fiery touches on the history of that face and his life. 'Older, of course. They are the features, of course. The likeness is not bad. I suppose it resembles her as she is now, or was when it was painted. You're an odd fellow to have asked for it.'

'I thought you would wish to have it, Philip.'

'You're a good boy, Patrice. Light those candles we'll go to bed. I want a cool head for such brains as I have, and bumping the pillow all night is not exactly wholesome. We'll cross the Channel in a few days, and see the nest, and the mother, and the girls.'

'Not St. George's Channel. Mother would rather you would go to France and visit the De Reuils. She and the girls hope you will keep out of Ireland for a time: it's hot. Judge if they're anxious, when it's to stop them from seeing you, Philip!'

'Good-night, dear boy.' Philip checked the departing Patrick. 'You can leave that.' He made a sign for the miniature to be left on the table.

Patrick laid it there. His brother had not touched it, and he could have defended himself for having forgotten to leave it, on the plea that it might prevent his brother from having his proper share of sleep; and also, that Philip had no great pleasure in the possession of it. The two pleas, however, did not make one harmonious apology, and he went straight to the door in an odd silence, with the step of a decorous office-clerk, keeping his shoulders turned on Philip to conceal his look of destitution.

CHAPTER XI. INTRODUCING A NEW CHARACTER

Letters and telegrams and morning journals lay on the breakfast-table, awaiting the members of the household with combustible matter. Bad news from Ireland came upon ominous news from India. Philip had ten words of mandate from his commanding officer, and they signified action, uncertain where. He was the soldier at once, buckled tight and buttoned up over his private sentiments. Vienna shot a line to Mrs. Adister O'Donnell. She communicated it:'The Princess Nikolas has a son!' Captain Con tossed his newspaper to the floor, crying:

'To-day the city'll be a chimney on fire, with the blacks in everybody's faces; but I must go down. It's hen and chicks with the director of a City Company. I must go.'

Did you say, madam?' Patrick inquired. 'A son,' said Mrs. Adister.

'And the military holloaing for reinforcements,' exclaimed Con. 'Pheu! Phil!'

'That's what it comes to,' was Philip's answer. 'Precautionary measures, eh?'

'You can make them provocative.' 'Will you beg for India?' 'I shall hear in an hour.' 'Have we got men?'

'Always the question with us.'

'What a country!' sighed the captain. 'I'd compose ye a song of old Drowsylid, except that it does no good to be singing it at the only time when you can show her the consequences of her sluggery. A country of compromise goes to pieces at the first cannon-shot of the advance, and while she's fighting on it's her poor business to be putting herself together again: So she makes a mess of the beginning, to a certainty. If it weren't that she had the army of Neptune about her—'

'The worst is she may some day start awake to discover that her protecting deity 's been napping too.—A boy or girl did you say, my dear?'

His wife replied: 'A son.'

'Ah! more births.' The captain appeared to be computing. 'But this one's out of England: and it's a prince I suppose they'll call him: and princes don't count in the population for more than finishing touches, like the crossing of t's and dotting of i's, though true they're the costliest, like some flowers and feathers, and they add to the lump on Barney's back. But who has any compassion for a burdened donkey? unless when you see him standing immortal meek! Well, and a child of some sort must have been expected? Because it's no miracle after marriage: worse luck for the crowded earth!'

'Things may not be expected which are profoundly distasteful,' Mrs. Adister remarked.

'True,' said her sympathetic husband. "Tis like reading the list of the dead after a battle where you've not had the best of it—each name 's a startling new blow. I'd offer to run to Earlsfont, but here's my company you would have me join for the directoring of it, you know, my dear, to ballast me, as you pretty clearly hinted; and all 's in the city to-day like a loaf with bad yeast, thick as lead, and sour to boot. And a howl and growl coming off the wilds of Old Ireland! We're smitten to-day in our hearts and our pockets, and it 's a question where we ought to feel it most, for the sake of our families.'

'Do you not observe that your cousins are not eating?' said his wife, adding, to Patrick: 'I entertain the opinion that a sound breakfast-appetite testifies to the proper vigour of men.'

'Better than a doctor's pass: and to their habits likewise,' Captain Con winked at his guests, begging them to steal ten minutes out of the fray for the inward fortification of them.

Eggs in the shell, and masses of eggs, bacon delicately thin and curling like Apollo's locks at his temples, and cutlets, caviar, anchovies in the state of oil, were pressed with the captain's fervid illustrations upon the brothers, both meditatively nibbling toast and indifferent to the similes he drew and applied to life from the little fish which had their sharpness corrected but not cancelled by the improved liquid they swam in. 'Like an Irishman in clover,' he said to his wife to pay her a compliment and coax an acknowledgement: 'just the flavour of the salt of him.'

Her mind was on her brother Edward, and she could not look sweet-oily, as her husband wooed her to do, with impulse to act the thing he was imagining.

'And there is to-morrow's dinner-party to the Mattocks: I cannot travel to Earlsfont,' she said.

'Patrick is a disengaged young verderer, and knows the route, and has a welcome face there, and he might go, if you're for having it performed by word of mouth. But, trust me, my dear, bad news is best communicated by telegraph, which gives us no stupid articles and particles to quarrel with. "Boy born Vienna doctor smiling nurse laughing." That tells it all, straight to the understanding, without any sickly circumlocutory stuff; and there's nothing more offensive to us when we're hurt at intelligence. For the same reason, Colonel Arthur couldn't go, since you'll want him to meet the Mattocks?'

Captain Con's underlip shone with a roguish thinness.

'Arthur must be here,' said Mrs. Adister. 'I cannot bring myself to write it. I disapprove of telegrams.'

She was asking to be assisted, so her husband said:

'Take Patrick for a secretary. Dictate. He has a bold free hand and'll supply all the fiorituri and arabesques necessary to the occasion running.'

She gazed at Patrick as if to intimate that he might be enlisted, and said: 'It will be to Caroline. She will break it to her uncle.'

'Right, madam, on the part of a lady I've never known to be wrong! And so, my dear, I must take leave of you, to hurry down to the tormented intestines of that poor racked city, where the winds of panic are violently engaged in occupying the vacuum created by knocking over what the disaster left standing; and it 'll much resemble a colliery accident there, I suspect, and a rescue of dead bodies. Adieu, my dear.' He pressed his lips on her thin fingers.

Patrick placed himself at Mrs. Adister's disposal as her secretary. She nodded a gracious acceptance of him.

'I recommended the telegraph because it's my wife's own style, and comes better from wires,' said the captain, as they were putting on their overcoats in the hall. 'You must know the family. "Deeds not words" would serve for their motto. She hates writing, and doesn't much love talking. Pat 'll lengthen her sentences for her. She's fond of Adiante, and she sympathises with her brother Edward made a grandfather through the instrumentality of that foreign hooknose; and Patrick must turn the two dagger sentiments to a sort of love-knot and there's the task he'll have to work out in his letter to Miss Caroline. It's fun about Colonel Arthur not going. He's to meet the burning Miss Mattock, who has gold on her crown and a lot on her treasury, Phil, my boy! but I'm bound in honour not to propose it. And a nice girl, a prize; afresh healthy girl; and brains: the very girl! But she's jotted down for the Adisters, if Colonel Arthur can look lower than his nose and wag his tongue a bit. She's one to be a mother of stout ones that won't run up big doctors' bills or ask assistance in growing. Her name's plain Jane, and she 's a girl to breed conquerors; and the same you may say of her brother John, who 's a mighty fit man, good at most things, though he counts his fortune in millions, which I've heard is lighter for a beggar to perform than in pounds, but he can count seven, and beat any of us easy by showing them millions! We might do something for them at home with a million or two, Phil. It all came from the wedding of a railway contractor, who sprang from the wedding of a spade and a clod—and probably called himself Mattock at his birth, no shame to him.'

'You're for the city,' said Philip, after they had walked down the street.

'Not I,' said Con. 'Let them play Vesuvius down there. I've got another in me: and I can't stop their eruption, and they wouldn't relish mine. I know a little of Dick Martin, who called on the people to resist, and housed the man Liffey after his firing the shot, and I'm off to Peter M'Christy, his brother-in-law. I'll see Distell too. I must know if it signifies the trigger, or I'm agitated about nothing. Dr. Forbery'll be able to tell how far they mean going for a patriotic song. Will you come, Phil?'

'I 'm under orders.'

'You won't engage yourself by coming.'

'I'm in for the pull if I join hands.'

'And why not?—inside the law, of course.'

'While your Barney skirmishes outside!'

'And when the poor fellow's cranium's cracking to fling his cap in the air, and physician and politician are agreed it's good for him to do it, or he'll go mad and be a dangerous lunatic! Phil, it must be a blow now and then for these people over here, else there's no teaching their imaginations you're in earnest; for they've got heads that open only to hard raps, these English; and where injustice rules, and you'd spread a light of justice, a certain lot of us must give up the ghost—naturally on both sides. Law's law, and life's life, so long as you admit that the law is bad; and in that case, it's big misery and chronic disease to let it be and at worst a jump and tumble into the next world, of a score or two of us if we have a wrestle with him. But shake the old villain; hang on him and shake him. Bother his wig, if he calls himself Law. That 's how we dust the corruption out of him for a bite or two in return. Such is humanity, Phil: and you must allow for the roundabout way of moving to get into the straight road at last. And I see what you're for saying: a roundabout eye won't find it! You're wrong where there are dozens of corners. Logic like yours, my boy, would have you go on picking at the Gordian Knot till it became a jackasses' race between you and the rope which was to fall to pieces last.—There 's my old girl at the stall, poor soul! See her!'

Philip had signalled a cabman to stop. He stood facing his cousin with a close-lipped smile that summarised his opinion and made it readable.

'I have no time for an introduction to her this morning,' he said.

'You won't drop in on Distell to hear the latest brewing? And, by the by, Phil, tell us, could you give us a hint for packing five or six hundred rifles and a couple of pieces of cannon?'

Philip stared; he bent a lowering frown on his cousin, with a twitch at his mouth.

'Oh! easy!' Con answered the look; 'it's for another place and harder to get at.'

He was eyed suspiciously and he vowed the military weapons were for another destination entirely, the opposite Pole.

'No, you wouldn't be in for a crazy villainy like that!' said Philip.

'No, nor wink to it,' said Con. 'But it's a question about packing cannon and small arms; and you might be useful in dropping a hint or two. The matter's innocent. It's not even a substitution of one form of Government for another: only a change of despots, I suspect. And here's Mr. John Mattock himself, who'll corroborate me, as far as we can let you into the secret before we've consulted together. And he's an Englishman and a member of Parliament, and a Liberal though a landlord, a thorough stout Briton and bulldog for the national integrity, not likely to play at arms and ammunition where his country's prosperity 's concerned. How d' ye do, Mr. Mattock—and opportunely, since it's my cousin, Captain Philip O'Donnell, aide-de-camp to Sir Charles, fresh from Canada, of whom you've heard, I'd like to make you acquainted with, previous to your meeting at my wife's table tomorrow evening.'

Philip bowed to a man whose notion of the ceremony was to nod.

Con took him two steps aside and did all the talking. Mr. Mattock listened attentively the first half-minute, after which it could be perceived that the orator was besieging a post, or in other words a Saxon's mind made up on a point of common sense. His appearance was redolently marine; his pilot coat, flying necktie and wideish trowsers, a general airiness of style on a solid frame, spoke of the element his blue eyes had dipped their fancy in, from hereditary inclination. The colour of a sandpit was given him by hair and whiskers of yellow-red on a ruddy face. No one could express a negative more emphatically without wording it, though he neither frowned nor gesticulated to that effect.

'Ah!' said Con, abruptly coming to an end after an eloquent appeal. 'And I think I'm of your opinion: and the sea no longer dashes at the rock, but makes itself a mirror to the same. She'll keep her money and nurse her babe, and not be trying risky adventures to turn him into a reigning prince. Only this: you'll have to persuade her the thing is impossible. She'll not take it from any of us. She looks on you as Wisdom in the uniform of a great commander, and if you say a thing can be done it 's done.'

'The reverse too, I hope,' said Mr. Mattock, nodding and passing on his way.

'That I am not so sure of,' Con remarked to himself. 'There's a change in a man through a change in his position! Six months or so back, Phil, that man came from Vienna, the devoted slave of the Princess Nikolas. He'd been there on his father's business about one of the Danube railways, and he was ready to fill the place of the prince at the head of his phantom body of horse and foot and elsewhere. We talked of his selling her estates for the purchase of arms and the enemy—as many as she had money for. We discussed it as a matter of business. She had bewitched him: and would again, I don't doubt, if she were here to repeat the dose. But in the interim his father dies, he inherits; and he enters Parliament, and now, mind you, the man who solemnly calculated her chances and speculates on the transmission of rifled arms of the best manufacture and latest invention by his yacht and with his loads of rails, under the noses of the authorities, like a master rebel, and a chivalrous gentleman to boot, pooh poohs the whole affair. You saw him. Grave as an owl, the dead contrary of his former self!'

'I thought I heard you approve him,' said Philip.

'And I do. But the poor girl has ordered her estates to be sold to cast the die, and I 'm taking the view of her disappointment, for she believes he can do anything; and if I know the witch, her sole comfort lying in the straw is the prospect of a bloody venture for a throne. The truth is, to my thinking, it's the only thing she has to help her to stomach her husband.'

'But it's rank idiocy to suppose she can smuggle cannon!' cried Philip.

'But that man Mattock's not an idiot and he thought she could. And it 's proof he was under a spell. She can work one.'

'The country hasn't a port.'

'Round the Euxine and up the Danube, with the British flag at the stern. I could rather enjoy the adventure. And her prince is called for. He's promised a good reception when he drops down the river, they say. A bit of a scrimmage on the landing-pier may be, and the first field or two, and then he sits himself, and he waits his turn. The people change their sovereigns as rapidly as a London purse. Two pieces of artillery and two or three hundred men and a trumpet alter the face of the land there. Sometimes a trumpet blown by impudence does it alone. They're enthusiastic for any new prince. He's their Weekly Journal or Monthly Magazine. Let them make acquaintance with Adiante Adister, I'd not swear she wouldn't lay fast hold of them.'

Philip signalled to his driver, and Captain Con sang out his dinner-hour for a reminder to punctuality, thoughtful of the feelings of his wife.

CHAPTER XII. MISS MATTOCK

Mrs. Adister O'Donnell, in common with her family, had an extreme dislike of the task of composing epistles, due to the circumstance that she was unable, unaided, to conceive an idea disconnected with the main theme of her communication, and regarded, as an art of conjuring, the use of words independent of ideas. Her native superiority caused her to despise the art, but the necessity for employing it at intervals subjected her to fits of admiration of the conjurer, it being then evident that a serviceable piece of work, beyond her capacity to do, was lightly performed by another. The lady's practical intelligence admitted the service, and at the same time her addiction to the practical provoked disdain of so flimsy a genius, which was identified by her with the genius of the Irish race. If Irishmen had not been notoriously fighters, famous for their chivalry, she would have looked on them as a kind of footmen hired to talk and write, whose volubility might be encouraged and their affectionateness deserved by liberal wages. The promptitude of Irish blood to deliver the war-cry either upon a glove flung down or taken up, raised them to a first place in her esteem: and she was a peaceful woman abhorring sanguinary contention; but it was in her own blood to love such a disposition against her principles.

She led Patrick to her private room, where they both took seats and he selected a pen. Mr. Patrick supposed that his business would be to listen and put her words to paper; a mechanical occupation permitting the indulgence of personal phantasies; and he was flying high on them until the extraordinary delicacy of the mind seeking to deliver itself forced him to prick up all his apprehensiveness. She wished to convey that she was pleased with the news from Vienna, and desired her gratification to be imparted to her niece Caroline, yet not so as to be opposed to the peculiar feelings of her brother Edward, which had her fullest sympathy; and yet Caroline must by no means be requested to alter a sentence referring to Adiante, for that would commit her and the writer jointly to an insincerity.

'It must be the whole truth, madam,' said Patrick, and he wrote: 'My dear Caroline,' to get the start. At once a magnificently clear course for the complicated letter was distinguished by him. 'Can I write on and read it to you afterward? I have the view,' he said.

Mrs. Adister waved to him to write on.

Patrick followed his 'My dear Caroline' with greetings very warm, founded on a report of her flourishing good looks. The decision of Government to send reinforcements to Ireland was mentioned as a prelude to the information from Vienna of the birth of a son to the Princess Nikolas: and then; having conjoined the two entirely heterogeneous pieces of intelligence, the composer adroitly interfused them by a careless transposition of the prelude and the burden that enabled him to play ad libitum on regrets and rejoicings; by which device the lord of Earlsfont might be offered condolences while the lady could express her strong contentment, inasmuch as he deplored the state of affairs in the sister island, and she was glad of a crisis concluding a term of suspense thus the foreign-born baby was denounced and welcomed, the circumstances lamented and the mother congratulated, in a breath, all under cover of the happiest misunderstanding, as effective as the cabalism of Prospero's wand among the Neapolitan mariners, by the skilful Irish development on a grand scale of the rhetorical figure anastrophe, or a turning about and about.

He read it out to her, enjoying his composition and pleased with his reconcilement of differences. 'So you say what you feel yourself, madam, and allow for the feelings on the other side,' he remarked. 'Shall I fold it?'

There was a smoothness in the letter particularly agreeable to her troubled wits, but with an awful taste. She hesitated to assent: it seemed like a drug that she was offered.

Patrick sketched a series of hooked noses on the blotter. He heard a lady's name announced at the door, and glancing up from his work he beheld a fiery vision.

Mrs. Adister addressed her affectionately: 'My dear Jane!' Patrick was introduced to Miss Mattock.

His first impression was that the young lady could wrestle with him and render it doubtful of his keeping his legs. He was next engaged in imagining that she would certainly burn and be a light in the dark. Afterwards he discovered her feelings to be delicate, her looks pleasant. Thereupon came one of the most singular sensations he had ever known: he felt that he was unable to see the way to please her. She confirmed it by her remarks and manner of speaking. Apparently she was conducting a business.

'You're right, my dear Mrs. Adister, I'm on my way to the Laundry, and I called to get Captain Con to drive there with me and worry the manageress about the linen they turn out: for gentlemen are complaining of their shirt-fronts, and if we get a bad name with them it will ruin us. Women will listen to a man. I hear he has gone down to the city. I must go and do it alone. Our accounts are flourishing, I'm glad to say, though we cannot yet afford to pay for a secretary, and we want one. John and I verified them last night. We're aiming at steam, you know. In three or four years we may found a steam laundry on our accumulated capital. If only we can establish it on a scale to let us give employment to at least as many women as we have working now! That is what I want to hear of. But if we wait for a great rival steam laundry to start ahead of us, we shall be beaten and have to depend on the charitable sentiments of rich people to support the Institution. And that won't do. So it's a serious question with us to think of taking the initiative: for steam must come. It's a scandal every day that it doesn't while we have coal. I'm for grand measures. At the same time we must not be imprudent: turning off hands, even temporarily, that have to feed infants, would be quite against my policy.'

Her age struck Patrick as being about twenty-three.

'Could my nephew Arthur be of any use to you?' said Mrs. Adister.

'Colonel Adister?' Miss Mattock shook her head. 'No.'

'Arthur can be very energetic when he takes up a thing.' 'Can he? But, Mrs. Adister, you are looking a little troubled. Sometimes you confide in me. You are so good to us with your subscriptions that I always feel in your debt.'

Patrick glanced at his hostess for a signal to rise and depart.

She gave none, but at once unfolded her perplexity, and requested Miss Mattock to peruse the composition of Mr. Patrick O'Donnell and deliver an opinion upon it.

The young lady took the letter without noticing its author. She read it through, handed it back, and sat with her opinion evidently formed within.

'What do you think of it?' she was asked.

'Rank jesuitry,' she replied.

'I feared so!' sighed Mrs. Adister. 'Yet it says everything I wish to have said. It spares my brother and it does not belie me. The effect of a letter is often most important. I cannot but consider this letter very ingenious. But the moment I hear it is jesuitical I forswear it. But then my dilemma remains. I cannot consent to give pain to my brother Edward: nor will I speak an untruth, though it be to save him from a wound. I am indeed troubled. Mr. Patrick, I cannot consent to despatch a jesuitical letter. You are sure of your impression, my dear Jane?'

'Perfectly,' said Miss Mattock.

Patrick leaned to her. 'But if the idea in the mind of the person supposed to be writing the letter is accurately expressed? Does it matter, if we call it jesuitical, if the emotion at work behind it happens to be a trifle so, according to your definition?'

She rejoined: 'I should say, distinctly it matters.'

'Then you'd not express the emotions at all?'

He flashed a comical look of astonishment as he spoke. She was not to be diverted; she settled into antagonism.

'I should write what I felt.'

'But it might be like discharging a bullet.'

'How?'

'If your writing in that way wounded the receiver.'

'Of course I should endeavour not to wound!'

'And there the bit of jesuitry begins. And it's innocent while it 's no worse than an effort to do a disagreeable thing as delicately as you can.'

She shrugged as delicately as she could:

'We cannot possibly please everybody in life.'

'No: only we may spare them a shock: mayn't we?'

'Sophistries of any description, I detest.'

'But sometimes you smile to please, don't you?'

'Do you detect falseness in that?' she answered, after the demurest of pauses.

'No: but isn't there a soupçon of sophistry in it?'

'I should say that it comes under the title of common civility.'

'And on occasion a little extra civility is permitted!'

'Perhaps: when we are not seeking a personal advantage.'

'On behalf of the Steam Laundry?'

Miss Mattock grew restless: she was too serious in defending her position to submit to laugh, and his goodhumoured face forbade her taking offence.

'Well, perhaps, for that is in the interest of others.'

'In the interests of poor and helpless females. And I agree with you with all my heart. But you would not be so considerate for the sore feelings of a father hearing what he hates to hear as to write a roundabout word to soften bad news to him?'

She sought refuge in the reply that nothing excused jesuitry.

'Except the necessities of civilisation,' said Patrick.

'Politeness is one thing,' she remarked pointedly.

'And domestic politeness is quite as needful as popular, you'll admit. And what more have we done in the letter than to be guilty of that? And people declare it's rarer: as if we were to be shut up in families to tread on one another's corns! Dear me! and after a time we should be having rank jesuitry advertised as the specific balsam for an unhappy domesticated population treading with hard heels from desperate habit and not the slightest intention to wound.'

'My dear Jane,' Mrs. Adister interposed while the young lady sat between mildly staring and blinking, 'you have, though still of a tender age, so excellent a head that I could trust to your counsel blindfolded. It is really deep concern for my brother. I am also strongly in sympathy with my niece, the princess, that beautiful Adiante: and my conscience declines to let me say that I am not.'

'We might perhaps presume to beg for Miss Mattock's assistance in the composition of a second letter more to her taste,' Patrick said slyly.

The effect was prompt: she sprang from her seat.

'Dear Mrs. Adister! I leave it to you. I am certain you and Mr. O'Donnell know best. It's too difficult and delicate for me. I am horribly blunt. Forgive me if I seemed to pretend to casuistry. I am sure I had no such meaning. I said what I thought. I always do. I never meant that it was not a very clever letter; and if it does exactly what you require it should be satisfactory. To-morrow evening John and I dine with you, and I look forward to plenty of controversy and amusement. At present I have only a head for work.'

'I wish I had that,' said Patrick devoutly.

She dropped her eyes on him, but without letting him perceive that he was a step nearer to the point of pleasing her.

CHAPTER XIII. THE DINNER-PARTY: Miss Mattock ventured on a prediction in her mind:

She was sure the letter would go. And there was not much to signify if it did. But the curious fatality that a person of such a native uprightness as Mrs. Adister should have been drawn in among Irishmen, set her thoughts upon the composer of the letter, and upon the contrast of his ingenuous look with the powerful cast of his head. She fancied a certain danger about him; of what kind she could not quite distinguish, for it had no reference to woman's heart, and he was too young to be much of a politician, and he was not in the priesthood. His transparency was of a totally different order from Captain Con's, which proclaimed itself genuine by the inability to conceal a shoal of subterfuges. The younger cousin's features carried a something invisible behind them, and she was just perceptive enough to spy it, and it excited her suspicions. Irishmen both she and her brother had to learn to like, owing to their bad repute for stability: they are, moreover, Papists: they are not given to ideas: that one of the working for the future has not struck them. In fine, they are not solid, not law-supporting, not disposed to be (humbly be it said) beneficent, like the good English. These were her views, and as she held it a weakness to have to confess that Irishmen are socially more fascinating than the good English, she was on her guard against them.

Of course the letter had gone. She heard of it before the commencement of the dinner, after Mrs. Adister had introduced Captain Philip O'Donnell to her, and while she was exchanging a word or two with Colonel Adister, who stood ready to conduct her to the table. If he addressed any remarks to the lady under his charge, Miss Mattock did not hear him; and she listened—who shall say why? His unlike likeness to his brother had struck her. Patrick opposite was flowing in speech. But Captain Philip O'Donnell's taciturnity seemed no uncivil gloom: it wore nothing of that look of being beneath the table, which some of our good English are guilty of at their social festivities, or of towering aloof a Matterhorn above it, in the style of Colonel Adister. Her discourse with the latter amused her passing reflections. They started a subject, and he punctuated her observations, or she his, and so they speedily ran to earth.

'I think,' says she, 'you were in Egypt this time last winter.'

He supplies her with a comma: 'Rather later.'

Then he carries on the line. 'Dull enough, if you don't have the right sort of travelling crew in your boat.'

'Naturally,' she puts her semicolon, ominous of the full stop.

'I fancy you have never been in Egypt?'

'No'

There it is; for the tone betrays no curiosity about Egypt and her Nile, and he is led to suppose that she has a distaste for foreign places.

Condescending to attempt to please, which he has reason to wish to succeed in doing, the task of pursuing conversational intercourse devolves upon him—

'I missed Parlatti last spring. What opinion have you formed of her?'

'I know her only by name at present.'
'Ah, I fancy you are indifferent to Opera.'
'Not at all; I enjoy it. I was as busy then as I am now.'
'Meetings? Dorcas, so forth.'
'Not Dorcas, I assure you. You might join if you would.'
'Your most obliged.'

A period perfectly rounded. At the same time Miss Mattock exchanged a smile with her hostess, of whose benignant designs in handing her to the entertaining officer she was not conscious. She felt bound to look happy to gratify an excellent lady presiding over the duller half of a table of eighteen. She turned slightly to Captain O'Donnell. He had committed himself to speech at last, without tilting his shoulders to exclude the company by devoting himself to his partner, and as he faced the table Miss Mattock's inclination to listen attracted him. He cast his eyes on her: a quiet look, neither languid nor frigid seeming to her both open and uninviting. She had the oddest little shiver, due to she knew not what. A scrutiny she could have borne, and she might have read a signification; but the look of those mild clear eyes which appeared to say nothing save that there was fire behind them, hit on some perplexity, or created it; for she was aware of his unhappy passion for the beautiful Miss Adister; the whole story had been poured into her ears; she had been moved by it. Possibly she had expected the eyes of such a lover to betray melancholy, and his power of containing the expression where the sentiment is imagined to be most transparent may have surprised her, thrilling her as melancholy orbs would not have done.

Captain Con could have thumped his platter with vexation. His wife's diplomacy in giving the heiress to Colonel Adister for the evening had received his cordial support while he manoeuvred cleverly to place Philip on the other side of her; and now not a step did the senseless fellow take, though she offered him his chance, dead sick of her man on the right; not a word did he have in ordinary civility; he was a burning disgrace to the chivalry of Erin. She would certainly be snapped up by a man merely yawning to take the bite. And there's another opportunity gone for the old country!—one's family to boot!

Those two were in the middle of the table, and it is beyond mortal, beyond Irish, capacity, from one end of a table of eighteen to whip up the whole body of them into a lively unanimous froth, like a dish of cream fetched out of thickness to the airiest lightness. Politics, in the form of a firebrand or apple of Discord, might knead them together and cut them in batches, only he had pledged his word to his wife to shun politics as the plague, considering Mr. Mattock's presence. And yet it was tempting: the recent Irish news had stung him; he could say sharp things from the heart, give neat thrusts; and they were fairly divided and well matched. There was himself, a giant; and there was an unrecognised bard of his country, no other than himself too; and there was a profound politician, profoundly hidden at present, like powder in a mine—the same person. And opposite to him was Mr. John Mattock, a worthy antagonist, delightful to rouse, for he carried big guns and took the noise of them for the shattering of the enemy, and this champion could be pricked on to a point of assertion sure to fire the phlegm in Philip; and then young

Patrick might be trusted to warm to the work. Three heroes out skirmishing on our side. Then it begins to grow hot, and seeing them at it in earnest, Forbery glows and couches his gun, the heaviest weight of the Irish light brigade. Gallant deeds! and now Mr. Marbury Dyke opens on Forbery's flank to support Mattock hardpressed, and this artillery of English Rockney resounds, with a similar object: the ladies to look on and award the crown of victory, Saxon though they be, excepting Rockney's wife, a sure deserter to the camp of the brave, should fortune frown on them, for a punishment to Rockney for his carrying off to himself a flower of the Green Island and holding inveterate against her native land in his black ingratitude. Oh! but eloquence upon a good cause will win you the hearts of all women, Saxon or other, never doubt of it. And Jane Mattock there, imbibing forced doses of Arthur Adister, will find her patriotism dissolving in the natural human current; and she and Philip have a pretty wrangle, and like one another none the worse for not agreeing: patriotically speaking, she's really unrooted by that half-thawed colonel, a creature snow-bound up to his chin; and already she's leaping to be transplanted. Jane is one of the first to give her vote for the Irish party, in spite of her love for her brother John: in common justice, she says, and because she hopes for complete union between the two islands. And thereupon we debate upon union. On the whole, yes: union, on the understanding that we have justice, before you think of setting to work to sow the land with affection:—and that's a crop in a clear soil will spring up harvest-thick in a single summer night across St. George's Channel, ladies!...

Indeed a goodly vision of strife and peace: but, politics forbidden, it was entirely a dream, seeing that politics alone, and a vast amount of blowing even on the topic of politics, will stir these English to enter the arena and try a fall. You cannot, until you say ten times more than you began by meaning, and have heated yourself to fancy you mean more still, get them into any state of fluency at all. Forbery's anecdote now and then serves its turn, but these English won't take it up as a start for fresh pastures; they lend their ears and laugh a finale to it; you see them dwelling on the relish, chewing the cud, by way of mental note for their friends to-morrow, as if they were kettles come here merely for boiling purposes, to make tea elsewhere, and putting a damper on the fire that does the business for them. They laugh, but they laugh extinguishingly, and not a bit to spread a general conflagration and illumination.

The case appeared hopeless to Captain Con, bearing an eye on Philip. He surveyed his inanimate eights right and left, and folded his combative ardour around him, as the soldier's martial cloak when he takes his rest on the field. Mrs. Marbury Dyke, the lady under his wing, honoured wife of the chairman of his imagined that a sigh escaped him, and said in sympathy: 'Is the bad news from India confirmed?'

He feared it was not bright, and called to Philip for the latest.

'Nothing that you have not had already in the newspapers,' Philip replied, distinctly from afar, but very bluntly, as through a trumpet.

Miss Mattock was attentive. She had a look as good as handsome when she kindled.

The captain persevered to draw his cousin out.

'Your chief has his orders?'

'There's a rumour to that effect.'

'The fellow's training for diplomacy,' Con groaned.

Philip spoke to Miss Mattock: he was questioned and he answered, and answered dead as a newspaper telegraphic paragraph, presenting simply the corpse of the fact, and there an end. He was a rival of Arthur Adister for military brevity.

'Your nephew is quite the diplomatist,' said Mrs. Dyke, admiring Philip's head.

'Cousin, ma'am. Nephews I might drive to any market to make the most of them. Cousins pretend they're better than pigs, and diverge bounding from the road at the hint of the stick. You can't get them to grunt more than is exactly agreeable to them.'

'My belief is that if our cause is just our flag will triumph,' Miss Grace Barrow, Jane Mattock's fellow-worker and particular friend, observed to Dr. Forbery.

'You may be enjoying an original blessing that we in Ireland missed in the cradle,' said he.

She emphasised: 'I speak of the just cause; it must succeed.'

'The stainless flag'll be in the ascendant in the long run,' he assented.

'Is it the flag of Great Britain you're speaking of, Forbery?' the captain inquired.

'There's a harp or two in it,' he responded pacifically.

Mrs. Dyke was not pleased with the tone. 'And never will be out of it!' she thumped her interjection.

'Or where's your music?' said the captain, twinkling for an adversary among the males, too distant or too dull to distinguish a note of challenge. 'You'd be having to mount your drum and fife in their places, ma'am.'

She saw no fear of the necessity.

'But the fife's a pretty instrument,' he suggested, and with a candour that seduced the unwary lady to think dubiously whether she quite liked the fife. Miss Barrow pronounced it cheerful.

'Oh, and martial!' he exclaimed, happy to have caught Rockney's deliberate gaze. 'The effect of it, I'm told in the provinces is astonishing for promoting enlistment. Hear it any morning in your London parks, at the head of a marching regiment of your giant foot-Guards. Three bangs of the drum, like the famous mountain, and the fife announces himself to be born, and they follow him, left leg and right leg and bearskin. And what if he's a small one and a trifle squeaky; so's a prince when the attendant dignitaries receive him submissively and hear him informing the nation of his advent. It's the idea that's grand.'

'The idea is everything in military affairs,' a solemn dupe, a Mr. Rumford, partly bald, of benevolent aspect, and looking more copious than his flow, observed to the lady beside him. 'The flag is only an idea.'

She protested against the barbarism of war, and he agreed with her, but thought it must be: it had always been: he deplored the fatality. Nevertheless, he esteemed our soldiers, our sailors too. A city man himself and a man of peace, he cordially esteemed and hailed the victories of a military body whose idea was Duty instead of Ambition.

'One thing,' said Mrs. Dyke, evading the ambiguous fife, 'patriotic as I am, I hope, one thing I confess; I never have yet brought myself to venerate thoroughly our Royal Standard. I dare say it is because I do not understand it.'

A strong fraternal impulse moved Mr. Rumford to lean forward and show her the face of one who had long been harassed by the same incapacity to digest that one thing. He guessed it at once, without a doubt of the accuracy of the shot. Ever since he was a child the difficulty had haunted him; and as no one hitherto had even comprehended his dilemma, he beamed like a man preparing to embrace a recovered sister.

'The Unicorn!' he exclaimed.

'It is the Unicorn!' she sighed. 'The Lion is noble.'

'The Unicorn, if I may speak by my own feelings, certainly does not inspire attachment, that is to say, the sense of devotion, which we should always be led to see in national symbols,' Mr. Rumford resumed, and he looked humorously rueful while speaking with some earnestness; to show that he knew the subject to be of the minor sort, though it was not enough to trip and jar a loyal enthusiasm in the strictly meditative.

'The Saxon should carry his White Horse, I suppose,' Dr. Forbery said.

'But how do we account for the horn on his forehead?' Mr. Rumford sadly queried.

'Two would have been better for the harmony of the Unicorn's appearance,' Captain Con remarked, desirous to play a floundering fish, and tender to the known simple goodness of the ingenuous man. 'What do you say, Forbery? The poor brute had a fall on his pate and his horn grew of it, and it 's to prove that he has got something in his head, and is dangerous both fore and aft, which is not the case with other horses, who're usually wicked at the heels alone. That's it, be sure, or near it. And his horn's there to file the subject nation's grievances for the Lion to peruse at his leisure. And his colour's prophetic of the Horse to come, that rides over all.'

'Lion and Unicorn signify the conquest of the two hemispheres, Matter and Mind,' said Dr. Forbery. 'The Lion there's no mistake about. The Unicorn sets you thinking. So it's a splendid Standard, and means the more for not being perfectly intelligible at a glance.'

'But if the Lion, as they've whispered of late, Forbery, happens to be stuffed with straw or with what's worse, with sawdust, a fellow bearing a pointed horn at close quarters might do him mortal harm; and it must be a situation trying to the patience of them both. The Lion seems to say "No prancing!" as if he knew his peril; and the Unicorn to threaten a playful dig at his flank, as if he understood where he's ticklish.'

Mr. Rumford drank some champagne and murmured with a shrug to the acquiescent lady beside him: 'Irishmen!' implying that the race could not be brought to treat serious themes as befitted the seriousness of the sentiments they stir in their bosoms. He was personally a little hurt, having unfolded a shy secret of his feelings, which were keenly patriotic in a phlegmatic frame, and he retired within himself, assuring the lady that he accepted our standard in its integrity; his objection was not really an objection; it was, he explained to her, a ridiculous desire to have a perfect comprehension of the idea in the symbol. But where there was no seriousness everything was made absurd. He could, he said, laugh as well as others on the proper occasion. As for the Lion being stuffed, he warned England's enemies for their own sakes not to be deluded by any such patent calumny. The strong can afford to be magnanimous and forbearing.

Only let not that be mistaken for weakness. A wag of his tail would suffice.

The lady agreed. But women are volatile. She was the next moment laughing at something she had heard with the largest part of her ear, and she thought the worthy gentleman too simple, though she knew him for one who had amassed wealth. Captain Con and Dr. Forbery had driven the Unicorn to shelter, and were now baiting the Lion. The tremendous import of that wag of his tail among the nations was burlesqued by them, and it came into collision with Mr. Rumford's legendary forefinger threat. She excused herself for laughing:

'They are so preposterous!'

'Yes, yes, I can laugh,' said he, soberly performing the act: and Mr. Rumford covered the wound his delicate sensations had experienced under an apology for Captain Con, that would redound to the credit of his artfulness were it not notorious our sensations are the creatures and born doctors of art in discovering unguents for healing their bruises. 'O'Donnell has a shrewd head for business. He is sound at heart. There is not a drop of gout in his wine.'

The lady laughed again, as we do when we are fairly swung by the tide, and underneath her convulsion she quietly mused on the preference she would give to the simple English citizen for soundness.

'What can they be discussing down there?' Miss Mattock said to Philip, enviously as poor Londoners in November when they receive letters from the sapphire Riviera.

'I will venture to guess at nonsense,' he answered.

'Nothing political, then.'

'That scarcely follows; but a host at his own table may be trusted to shelve politics.'

'I should not object.'

'To controversy?'

'Temperately conducted.'

'One would go a long way to see the exhibition.'

'But why cannot men be temperate in their political arguments?'

'The questions raised are too close about the roots of us.'

'That sounds very pessimist.'

'More duels come from politics than from any other source.'

'I fear it is true. Then women might set you an example.'

'By avoiding it?'

'I think you have been out of England for some time.'

'I have been in America.'

'We are not exactly on the pattern of the Americans.' Philip hinted a bow. He praised the Republican people.

'Yes, but in our own way we are working out our own problems over here,' said she. 'We have infinitely more to contend with: old institutions, monstrous prejudices, and a slower-minded people, I dare say: much slower, I admit. We are not shining to advantage at present. Still, that is not the fault of English women.'

'Are they so spirited?'

Spirited was hardly the word Miss Mattock would have chosen to designate the spirit in them. She hummed a second or two, deliberating; it flashed through her during the pause that he had been guilty of irony, and she reddened: and remembering a foregoing strange sensation she reddened more. She had been in her girlhood a martyr to this malady of youth; it had tied her to the stake and enveloped her in flames for no accountable reason, causing her to suffer cruelly and feel humiliated. She knew the pangs of it in public, and in private as well. And she had not conquered it yet. She was angered to find herself such a merely physical victim of the rushing blood: which condition of her senses did not immediately restore her natural colour.

'They mean nobly,' she said, to fill an extending gap in the conversation under a blush; and conscious of an ultra-swollen phrase, she snatched at it nervously to correct it: 'They are becoming alive to the necessity for action.' But she was talking to a soldier! 'I mean, their heads are opening.' It sounded ludicrous. 'They are educating themselves differently.' Were they? 'They wish to take their part in the work of the world.' That was nearer the proper tone, though it had a ring of claptrap rhetoric hateful to her: she had read it and shrunk from it in reports of otherwise laudable meetings.

'Well, spirited, yes. I think they are. I believe they are. One has need to hope so.'

Philip offered a polite affirmative, evidently formal.

Not a sign had he shown of noticing her state of scarlet. His grave liquid eyes were unalterable. She might have been grateful, but the reflection that she had made a step to unlock the antechamber of her dearest deepest matters to an ordinary military officer, whose notions of women were probably those of his professional brethren, impelled her to transfer his polished decorousness to the burden of his masculine antagonism-plainly visible. She brought the dialogue to a close. Colonel Adister sidled an eye at a three-quarter view of her face. 'I fancy you're feeling the heat of the room,' he said.

Jane acknowledged a sensibility to some degree of warmth.

The colonel was her devoted squire on the instant for any practical service. His appeal to his aunt concerning one of the windows was answered by her appeal to Jane's countenance for a disposition to rise and leave the gentlemen. Captain Con, holding the door for the passage of his wife and her train of ladies, received the injunction:

'Ten,' from her, and remarked: 'Minutes,' as he shut it. The shortness of the period of grace proposed dejection to him on the one hand, and on the other a stimulated activity to squeeze it for its juices without any delay. Winding past Dr. Forbery to the vacated seat of the hostess he frowned forbiddingly.

'It's I, is it!' cried the doctor. Was it ever he that endangered the peace and placability of social gatherings! He sat down prepared rather for a bout with Captain Con than with their common opponents, notwithstanding that he had accurately read the mock thunder of his brows.

CHAPTER XIV. OF ROCKNEY

Battles have been won and the streams of History diverted to new channels in the space of ten minutes. Ladies have been won, a fresh posterity founded, and grand financial schemes devised, revolts arranged, a yoke shaken off, in less of mortal time. Excepting an inspired Epic song and an original Theory of the Heavens, almost anything noteworthy may be accomplished while old Father Scythe is taking a trot round a courtyard; and those reservations should allow the splendid conception to pass for the performance, when we bring to mind that the conception is the essential part of it, as a bard poorly known to fame was constantly urging. Captain Con had blown his Epic bubbles, not to speak of his projected tuneful narrative of the adventures of the great Cuchullin, and his Preaching of St. Patrick, and other national triumphs. He could own, however, that the world had a right to the inspection of the Epic books before it awarded him his crown. The celestial Theory likewise would have to be worked out to the last figure by the illustrious astronomers to whom he modestly ranked himself second as a benefactor of his kind, revering him. So that, whatever we may think in our own hearts, Epic and Theory have to remain the exception. Battles indeed have been fought, but when you survey the field in preparation for them you are summoned to observe the preluding courtesies of civilised warfare in a manner becoming a chivalrous gentleman. It never was the merely flinging of your leg across a frontier, not even with the abrupt Napoleon. You have besides to drill your men; and you have often to rouse your foe with a ringing slap, if he's a sleepy one or shamming sleepiness. As here, for example: and that of itself devours more minutes than ten. Rockney and Mattock could be roused; but these English, slow to kindle, can't subside in a twinkling; they are for preaching on when they have once begun; betray the past engagement, and the ladies are chilled, and your wife puts you the pungent question: 'Did you avoid politics, Con?' in the awful solitude of domestic life after a party. Now, if only there had been freedom of discourse during the dinner hour, the ten disembarrassed minutes allotted to close it would have afforded time sufficient for hearty finishing blows and a soothing word or so to dear old innocent Mr. Rumford, and perhaps a kindly clap of the shoulder to John Mattock, no bad fellow at bottom. Rockney too was no bad fellow in his way. He wanted no more than a beating and a thrashing. He was a journalist, a hard-headed rascal, none of your good old-fashioned order of regimental scribes who take their cue from their colonel, and march this way and that, right about face, with as little impediment of principles to hamper their twists and turns as the straw he tosses aloft at midnight to spy the drift of the wind to-morrow. Quite the contrary; Rockney was his own colonel; he pretended to think independently, and tried to be the statesman of a leading article, and showed his intention to stem the current of liberty, and was entirely deficient in sympathy with the oppressed, a fanatical advocate of force; he was an inveterate Saxon, good-hearted and in great need of a drubbing. Certain lines Rockney had written of late about Irish affairs recurred to Captain Con, and the political fires leaped in him; he sparkled and said: 'Let me beg you to pass the claret over to Mr. Rockney, Mr. Rumford; I warrant it for the circulating medium of amity, if he'll try it.'

"Tis the Comet Margaux,' said Dr. Forbery, topping anything Rockney might have had to say, and anything would have served. The latter clasped the decanter, poured and drank in silence.

'Tis the doctor's antidote, and best for being antedated,' Captain Con rapped his friend's knuckles.

'As long as you're contented with not dating in double numbers,' retorted the doctor, absolutely scattering the precious minutes to the winds, for he hated a provocation.

'There's a golden mean, is there!'

'There is; there's a way between magnums of good wine and gout, and it's generally discovered too late.'

'At the physician's door, then! where the golden mean is generally discovered to be his fee. I've heard of poor souls packed off by him without an obolus to cross the ferry. Stripped they were in all conscience.'

'You remind me of a fellow in Dublin who called on me for medical advice, and found he'd forgotten his purse. He offered to execute a deed to bequeath me his body, naked and not ashamed.'

'You'd a right to cut him up at once, Forbery. Any Jury 'd have pronounced him guilty of giving up the ghost before he called.'

'I let him go, body and all. I never saw him again.'

'The fellow was not a lunatic. As for your golden mean, there's a saying: Prevention is better than cure: and another that caps it: Drink deep or taste not.'

'That's the Pierian Spring.'

'And what is the wine on my table, sir?'

'Exhaustless if your verses come of it.'

'And pure, you may say of the verses and the fount.'

'And neither heady nor over-composed; with a blush like Diana confessing her love for the young shepherd: it's one of your own comparisons.'

'Oh!' Con could have roared his own comparisons out of hearing. He was angry with Forbery for his obstructive dulness and would not taste the sneaking compliment. What could Forbery mean by paying compliments and spoiling a game! The ten minutes were dancing away like harmless wood-nymphs when the Satyr slumbers. His eyes ranged over his guests despondently, and fixed in desperation on Mr. Rumford, whom his magnanimous nature would have spared but for the sharp necessity to sacrifice him.

The wine in Rumford at any rate let loose his original nature, if it failed to unlock the animal in these other unexcitable Saxons.

'By the way, now I think of it, Mr. Rumford, the interpretation of your Royal Standard, which perplexes you so much, strikes me as easy if you 'll examine the powerfully different colours of the two beasts in it.'

Mr. Rumford protested that he had abandoned his inquiry: it was a piece of foolishness: he had no feeling in it whatever, none.

The man was a perfect snail's horn for coyness.

The circumstances did not permit of his being suffered to slip away: and his complexion showed that he might already be classed among the roast.

'Your Lion:—Mr. Rumford, you should know, is discomposed, as a thoughtful patriot, by the inexplicable presence of the Unicorn in the Royal Standard, and would be glad to account for his one horn and the sickly appearance of the beast. I'm prepared to say he's there to represent the fair one half of the population.

Your Lion, my dear sir, may have nothing in his head, but his tawniness tells us he imbibes good sound stuff, worthy of the reputation of a noble brewery. Whereas your Unicorn, true to the character of the numberless hosts he stands for, is manifestly a consumer of doctor's drugs. And there you have the symbolism of your country. Right or left of the shield, I forget which, and it is of no importance to the point—you have Grandgosier or Great Turk in all his majesty, mane and tail; and on the other hand, you behold, as the showman says, Dyspepsia. And the pair are intended to indicate that you may see yourselves complete by looking at them separately; and so your Royal Standard is your national mirror; and when you gaze on it fondly you're playing the part of a certain Mr. Narcissus, who got liker to the Lion than to the Unicorn in the act. Now will that satisfy you?'

'Quite as you please, quite as you please,' Mr. Rumford replied. 'One loves the banner of one's country—that is all.' He rubbed his hands. 'I for one am proud of it.'

'Far be it from me to blame you, my dear sir. Or there's the alternative of taking him to stand for your sole great festival holiday, and worshipping him as the personification of your Derbyshire race.'

A glittering look was in Captain Con's eye to catch Rockney if he would but rise to it.

That doughty Saxon had been half listening, half chatting to Mr. Mattock, and wore on his drawn eyelids and slightly drawn upper lip a look of lambent pugnacity awake to the challenge, indifferent to the antagonist, and disdainful of the occasion.

'We have too little of your enthusiasm for the flag,' Philip said to Mr. Rumford to soothe him, in a form of apology for his relative.

'Surely no! not in England?' said Mr. Rumford, tempted to open his heart, for he could be a bellicose gentleman by deputy of the flag. He recollected that the speaker was a cousin of Captain Con's, and withdrew into his wound for safety. 'Here and there, perhaps; not when we are roused; we want rousing, we greatly prefer to live at peace with the world, if the world will let us.'

'Not at any price?' Philip fancied his tone too quakerly.

'Indeed I am not one of that party!' said Mr. Rumford, beginning to glow; but he feared a snare, and his wound drew him in again.

'When are you ever at peace!' quoth his host, shocked by the inconsiderate punctuality of Mrs. Adister O'Donnell's household, for here was the coffee coming round, and Mattock and Rockney escaping without a scratch. 'There's hardly a day in the year when your scarlet mercenaries are not popping at niggers.'

Rockney had the flick on the cheek to his manhood now, it might be hoped.

'Our what?' asked Mr. Rumford, honestly unable to digest the opprobrious term.

'Paid soldiery, hirelings, executioners, whom you call volunteers, by a charming euphemism, and send abroad to do the work of war while you propound the doctrines of peace at home.'

Rockney's forehead was exquisitely eruptive, red and swelling. Mattock lurched on his chair. The wine was in them, and the captain commended the spiriting of it, as Prospero his Ariel.

Who should intervene at this instant but the wretched Philip, pricked on the point of honour as a soldier! Are we inevitably to be thwarted by our own people?

'I suppose we all work for pay,' said he. 'It seems to me a cry of the streets to call us by hard names. The question is what we fight for.'

He spoke with a witless moderation that was most irritating, considering the latest news from the old country.

'You fight to subjugate, to enslave,' said Con, 'that's what you're doing, and at the same time your journals are venting their fine irony at the Austrians and the Russians and the Prussians for tearing Poland to strips with their bloody beaks.'

'We obey our orders, and leave you to settle the political business,' Philip replied.

Forbery declined the fray. Patrick was eagerly watchful and dumb. Rockney finished his coffee with a rap of the cup in the saucer, an appeal for the close of the sitting; and as Dr. Forbery responded to it by pushing back his chair, he did likewise, and the other made a movement.

The disappointed hero of a fight unfought had to give the signal for rising. Double the number of the ten minutes had elapsed. He sprang up, hearing Rockney say: 'Captain Con O'Donnell is a politician or nothing,' and as he was the most placable of men concerning his personality, he took it lightly, with half a groan that it had not come earlier, and said, 'He thinks and he feels, poor fellow!'

All hope of a general action was over.

'That shall pass for the epitaph of the living,' said Rockney.

It was too late to catch at a trifle to strain it to a tussle. Con was obliged to subjoin: 'Inscribe it on the dungeon-door of tyranny.' But the note was peaceful.

He expressed a wish that the fog had cleared for him to see the stars of heaven before he went to bed, informing Mr. Mattock that a long look in among them was often his prayer at night, and winter a holy season to him, for the reason of its showing them bigger and brighter.

'I can tell my wife with a conscience we've had a quiet evening, and you're a witness to it,' he said to Patrick. That consolation remained.

'You know the secret of your happiness,' Patrick answered.

'Know you one of the secrets of a young man's fortune in life, and give us a thrilling song at the piano, my son,' said Con: 'though we don't happen to have much choice of virgins for ye to-night. Irish or French. Irish are popular. They don't mind having us musically. And if we'd go on joking to the end we should content them, if only by justifying their opinion that we're born buffoons.'

His happy conscience enabled him to court his wife with assiduity and winsomeness, and the ladies were once more elated by seeing how chivalrously lover-like an Irish gentleman can be after years of wedlock.

Patrick was asked to sing. Miss Mattock accompanied him at the piano. Then he took her place on the music-stool, and she sang, and with an electrifying splendour of tone and style.

'But it's the very heart of an Italian you sing with!' he cried.

'It will surprise you perhaps to hear that I prefer German music,' said she.

'But where—who had the honour of boasting you his pupil?'

She mentioned a famous master. Patrick had heard of him in Paris. He begged for another song and she complied, accepting the one he selected as the favourite of his brother Philip's, though she said: 'That one?' with a superior air. It was a mellifluous love-song from a popular Opera somewhat out of date. 'Well, it's in Italian!' she summed up her impressions of the sickly words while scanning them for delivery. She had no great admiration of the sentimental Sicilian composer, she confessed, yet she sang as if possessed by him. Had she, Patrick thought, been bent upon charming Philip, she could not have thrown more fire into the notes. And when she had done, after thrilling the room, there was a gesture in her dismissal of the leaves displaying critical loftiness. Patrick noticed it and said, with the thrill of her voice lingering in him: 'What is it you do like? I should so like to know.'

She was answering when Captain Con came up to the piano and remarked in an undertone to Patrick: 'How is it you hit on the song Adiante Adister used to sing?'

Miss Mattock glanced at Philip. He had applauded her mechanically, and it was not that circumstance which caused the second rush of scarlet over her face. This time she could track it definitely to its origin. A lover's favourite song is one that has been sung by his love. She detected herself now in the full apprehension of the fact before she had sung a bar: it had been a very dim fancy: and she denounced herself guilty of the knowledge that she was giving pain by singing the stuff fervidly, in the same breath that accused her of never feeling things at the right moment vividly. The reminiscences of those pale intuitions made them always affectingly vivid.

But what vanity in our emotional state in a great jarring world where we are excused for continuing to seek our individual happiness only if we ally it and subordinate it to the well being of our fellows! The interjection was her customary specific for the cure of these little tricks of her blood. Leaving her friend Miss Barrow at the piano, she took a chair in a corner and said; 'Now, Mr. O'Donnell, you will hear the music that moves me.'

'But it's not to be singing,' said Patrick. 'And how can you sing so gloriously what you don't care for? It puzzles me completely.'

She assured him she was no enigma: she hushed to him to hear.

He dropped his underlip, keeping on the conversation with his eyes until he was caught by the masterly playing of a sonata by the chief of the poets of sound.

He was caught by it, but he took the close of the introductory section, an allegro con brio, for the end, and she had to hush at him again, and could not resist smiling at her lullaby to the prattler. Patrick smiled in response. Exchanges of smiles upon an early acquaintance between two young people are peeps through the doorway of intimacy. She lost sight of the Jesuit. Under the influence of good music, too, a not unfavourable inclination towards the person sitting beside us and sharing that sweetness, will soften general prejudices—if he was Irish, he was boyishly Irish, not like his inscrutable brother; a better, or hopefuller edition of Captain Con; one with whom something could be done to steady him, direct him, improve him. He might be taught to appreciate Beethoven and work for his fellows. 'Now does not that touch you more deeply than the Italian?' said she, delicately mouthing: 'I, mio tradito amor!'

'Touch, I don't know,' he was honest enough to reply. 'It's you that haven't given it a fair chance I'd like to hear it again. There's a forest on fire in it.'

'There is,' she exclaimed. 'I have often felt it, but never seen it. You exactly describe it. How true!'

'But any music I could listen to all day and all the night,' said he.

'And be as proud of yourself the next morning?'

Patrick was rather at sea. What could she mean?

Mrs. Adister O'Donnell stepped over to them, with the object of installing Colonel Adister in Patrick's place.

The object was possibly perceived. Mrs. Adister was allowed no time to set the manoeuvre in motion.

'Mr. O'Donnell is a great enthusiast for music, and could listen to it all day and all night, he tells me,' said Miss Mattock. 'Would he not sicken of it in a week, Mrs. Adister?'

'But why should I?' cried Patrick. 'It's a gift of heaven.'

'And, like other gifts of heaven, to the idle it would turn to evil.'

'I can't believe it.'

'Work, and you will believe it.'

'But, Miss Mattock, I want to work; I'm empty-handed. It's true I want to travel and see a bit of the world to help me in my work by and by. I'm ready to try anything I can do, though.'

'Has it ever struck you that you might try to help the poor?'

'Arthur is really anxious, and only doubts his ability,' said Mrs. Adister.

'The doubt throws a shadow on the wish,' said Miss Mattock. 'And can one picture Colonel Adister the secretary of a Laundry Institution, receiving directions from Grace and me! We should have to release him long before the six months' term, when we have resolved to incur the expense of a salaried secretary.'

Mrs. Adister turned her head to the colonel, who was then looking down the features of Mrs. Rockney.

Patrick said: 'I'm ready, for a year, Miss Mattock.'

She answered him, half jocosely: 'A whole year of free service? Reflect on what you are undertaking.'

'It's writing and accounts, no worse?'

'Writing and accounts all day, and music in the evening only now and then.'

'I can do it: I will, if you'll have me.'

'Do you hear Mr. O'Donnell, Mrs. Adister?'

Captain Con fluttered up to his wife, and heard the story from Miss Mattock.

He fancied he saw a thread of good luck for Philip in it. 'Our house could be Patrick's home capitally,' he suggested to his wife. She was not a whit less hospitable, only hinting that she thought the refusal of the post was due to Arthur.

'And if he accepts, imagine him on a stool, my dear madam; he couldn't sit it!'

Miss Mattock laughed. 'No, that is not to be thought of seriously. And with Mr. O'Donnell it would be probationary for the first fortnight or month. Does he know anything about steam?'

'The rudimentary idea,' said Patrick.

'That's good for a beginning,' said the captain; and he added: 'Miss Mattock, I'm proud if one of my family can be reckoned worthy of assisting in your noble work.'

She replied: 'I warn everybody that they shall be taken at their word if they volunteer their services.'

She was bidden to know by the captain that the word of an Irish gentleman was his bond. 'And not later than to-morrow evening I'll land him at your office. Besides, he'll find countrywomen of his among you, and there's that to enliven him. You say they work well, diligently, intelligently.'

She deliberated. 'Yes, on the whole; when they take to their work. Intelligently certainly compared with our English. We do not get the best of them in London. For that matter, we do not get the best of the English—not the women of the north. We have to put up with the rejected of other and better-paying departments of work. It breaks my heart sometimes to see how near they are to doing well, but for such a little want of ballast.'

'If they're Irish,' said Patrick, excited by the breaking of her heart, 'a whisper of cajolery in season is often the secret.'

Captain Con backed him for diplomacy. 'You'll learn he has a head, Miss Mattock.'

'I am myself naturally blunt, and prefer the straightforward method,' said she.

Patrick nodded. 'But where there's an obstruction in the road, it's permissible to turn a corner.'

'Take 'em in flank when you can't break their centre,' said Con.

'Well, you shall really try whether you can endure the work for a short time if you are in earnest,' Miss Mattock addressed the volunteer.

'But I am,' he said.

'We are too poor at present to refuse the smallest help.'

'And mine is about the smallest.'

'I did not mean that, Mr. O'Donnell.'

'But you'll have me?'

'Gladly.'

Captain Con applauded the final words between them. They had the genial ring, though she accepted the wrong young man for but a shadow of the right sort of engagement.

This being settled, by the sudden combination of enthusiastic Irish impulse and benevolent English scheming, she very considerately resigned herself to Mrs. Adister's lead and submitted herself to a further jolting in the unprogressive conversational coach with Colonel Adister, whose fault as a driver was not in avoiding beaten ways, but whipping wooden horses.

Evidently those two were little adapted to make the journey of life together, though they were remarkably fine likenesses of a pair in the dead midway of the journey, Captain Con reflected, and he could have jumped at the thought of Patrick's cleverness: it was the one bright thing of the evening. There was a clear gain in it somewhere. And if there was none, Jane Mattock was a good soul worth saving. Why not all the benefaction on our side, and a figo for rewards! Devotees or adventurers, he was ready in imagination to see his cousins play the part of either, as the cross-roads offered, the heavens appeared to decree. We turn to the right or the left, and this way we're voluntary drudges, and that way we're lucky dogs; it's all according to the turn, the fate of it. But never forget that old Ireland is weeping!

He hummed the spontaneous lines. He was accused of singing to himself, and a song was vigorously demanded of him by the ladies.

He shook his head. 'I can't,' he sighed. 'I was plucking the drowned body of a song out of the waters to give it decent burial. And if I sing I shall be charged with casting a firebrand at Mr. Rockney.'

Rockney assured him that he could listen to anything in verse.

'Observe the sneer:—for our verses are smoke,' said Con.

Miss Mattock pressed him to sing.

But he had saddened his mind about old Ireland: the Irish news weighed heavily on him, unrelieved by a tussle with Rockney. If he sang, it would be an Irish song, and he would break down in it, he said; and he hinted at an objection of his wife's to spirited Irish songs of the sort which carry the sons of Erin bounding over the fences of tyranny and the brook of tears. And perhaps Mr. Rockney might hear a tale in verse as hard to bear as he sometimes found Irish prose!—Miss Mattock perceived that his depression was genuine, not less than his desire to please her. 'Then it shall be on another occasion,' she said.

'Oh! on another occasion I'm the lark to the sky, my dear lady.'

Her carriage was announced. She gave Patrick a look, with a smile, for it was to be a curious experiment. He put on the proper gravity of a young man commissioned, without a dimple of a smile. Philip bowed to her stiffly, as we bow to a commanding officer who has insulted us and will hear of it. But for that, Con would have manoeuvred against his wife to send him downstairs at the lady's heels. The fellow was a perfect riddle, hard to read as the zebra lines on the skin of a wild jackass—if Providence intended any meaning when she traced them! and it's a moot point: as it is whether some of our poets have meaning and are not composers of zebra. 'No one knows but them above!' he said aloud, apparently to his wife.

'What can you be signifying?' she asked him. She had deputed Colonel Arthur to conduct Miss Mattock and Miss Barrow to their carriage, and she supposed the sentence might have a mysterious reference to the plan she had formed; therefore it might be a punishable offence. Her small round eyes were wide-open, her head was up and high.

She was easily appeased, too easily.

'The question of rain, madam,' he replied to her repetition of his words. 'I dare say that was what I had in my mind, hearing Mr. Mattock and Mr. Rockney agree to walk in company to their clubs.'

He proposed to them that they should delay the march on a visit to his cabin near the clouds. They were forced to decline his invitation to the gentle lion's mouth; as did Mr. Rumford, very briskly and thankfully. Mr. Rockney was taken away by Mr. and Mrs. Marbury Dyke. So the party separated, and the Englishmen were together, and the Irishmen together; and hardly a syllable relating to the Englishmen did the Irishmen say, beyond an allusion to an accident to John Mattock's yacht off the Irish west-coast last autumn; but the Irishmen were subjected to some remarks by the Englishmen, wherein their qualities as individuals and specimens of a race were critically and neatly packed. Common sense is necessarily critical in its collision with vapours, and the conscious possessors of an exclusive common sense are called on to deliver a summary verdict, nor is it an unjust one either, if the verdict be taken simply for an estimate of what is presented upon the plain surface of to-day. Irishmen are queer fellows, never satisfied, thirsting for a shindy. Some of them get along pretty well in America. The air of their Ireland intoxicates them. They require the strong hand: fair legislation, but no show of weakness. Once let them imagine you are afraid of them, and they see perfect independence in their grasp. And what would be the spectacle if they were to cut themselves loose from England? The big ship might be inconvenienced by the loss of the tender; the tender would fall adrift on the Atlantic, with pilot and captain at sword and pistol, the crew playing Donnybrook freely. Their cooler heads are shrewd enough to see the folly, but it catches the Irish fancy to rush to the extreme, and we have allowed it to be supposed that it frightens us. There is the capital blunder, fons et origo.

Their leaders now pretend to work upon the Great Scale; they demand everything on the spot upon their own interpretation of equity. Concessions, hazy speeches, and the puling nonsense of our present Government, have encouraged them so far and got us into the mess. Treat them as policemen treat highwaymen: give them the law: and the law must be tightened, like the hold on a rogue by his collar, if they kick at it. Rockney was for sharp measures in repression, fair legislation in due course.

'Fair legislation upon your own interpretation of fair,' said Mattock, whose party opposed Rockney's. 'As to repression, you would have missed that instructive scene this evening at Con O'Donnell's table, if you had done him the kindness to pick up his glove. It 's wisest to let them exhaust their energies upon one another. Hold off, and they're soon at work.'

'What kind of director of a City Company does he make?' said Rockney.

Mattock bethought him that, on the whole, strange to say, Con O'Donnell comported himself decorously as a director, generally speaking on the reasonable side, not without shrewdness: he seemed to be sobered by the money question.

'That wife of his is the salvation of him,' Rockney said, to account for the Captain's shrewdness. 'She manages him cleverly. He knows the length of his line. She's a woman of principle, and barring the marriage, good sense too. His wife keeps him quiet, or we should be hearing of him. Forbery 's a more dangerous man. There's no intentional mischief in Con O'Donnell; it's only effervescence. I saw his game, and declined to uncork him. He talks of a niece of his wife's: have you ever seen her?—married to some Servian or Roumanian prince.'

Mattock answered: 'Yes.'

'Is she such a beauty?'

Again Mattock answered: 'Yes,' after affecting thoughtfulness.

'They seem to marry oddly in that family.'

Mattock let fly a short laugh at the remark, which had the ring of some current phrase. 'They do,' he said.

Next morning Jane Mattock spoke to her brother of her recruit. He entirely trusted to her discretion; the idea of a young Irish secretary was rather comical, nevertheless. He had his joke about it, requesting to have a sight of the secretary's books at the expiry of the week, which was the length of time he granted this ardent volunteer for evaporating and vanishing.

'If it releases poor Grace for a week, it will be useful to us,' Jane said. 'Women are educated so shamefully that we have not yet found one we can rely on as a competent person. And Mr. O'Donnell—did you notice him? I told you I met him a day or two back—seems willing to be of use. It cannot hurt him to try. Grace has too much on her hands.'

'She has a dozen persons.'

'They are zealous when they are led.'

'Beware of letting them suspect that they are led.'

'They are anxious to help the poor if they can discover how.'

'Good men, I don't doubt,' said John Mattock. 'Any proposals from curates recently?'

'Not of late. Captain O'Donnell, the brother of our secretary, is handsomer, but we do not think him so trustworthy. Did you observe him at all?—he sat by me. He has a conspirator's head.'

'What is that?' her brother asked her.

'Only a notion of mine.'

She was directed to furnish a compendious report of the sayings, doings, and behaviour of the Irish secretary in the evening.

'If I find him there,' she said.

Her brother was of opinion that Mr. Patrick O'Donnell would be as good as his word, and might be expected to appear there while the novelty lasted.

CHAPTER XV. THE MATTOCK FAMILY

That evening's report of the demeanour of the young Irish secretary in harness was not so exhilarating as John Mattock had expected, and he inclined to think his sister guilty of casting her protecting veil over the youth. It appeared that Mr. O'Donnell had been studious of his duties, had spoken upon no other topic, had asked pertinent questions, shown no flippancy, indulged in no extravagances. He seemed, Jane said, eager to master details. A certain eagerness of her own in speaking of it sharpened her clear features as if they were cutting through derision. She stated it to propitiate her brother, as it might have done but for the veracious picture of Patrick in the word 'eager,' which pricked the scepticism of a practical man. He locked his mouth, looking at her with a twinkle she refused to notice. 'Determined to master details' he could have accepted. One may be determined to find a needle in a dust-heap; one does not with any stiffness of purpose go at a dust-heap eagerly. Hungry men have eaten husks; they have not betrayed eagerness for such dry stuff. Patrick's voracity after details exhibited a doubtfully genuine appetite, and John deferred his amusement until the termination of the week or month when his dear good Jane would visit the office to behold a vacated seat, or be assailed by the customary proposal. Irishmen were not likely to be far behind curates in besieging an heiress. For that matter, Jane was her own mistress and could very well take care of herself; he had confidence in her wisdom.

He was besides of an unsuspicious and an unexacting temperament. The things he would strongly object to he did not specify to himself because he was untroubled by any forethought of them. Business, political, commercial and marine, left few vacancies in his mind other than for the pleasures he could command and enjoy. He surveyed his England with a ruddy countenance, and saw the country in the reflection. His England saw much of itself in him. Behind each there was more, behind the country a great deal more, than could be displayed by a glass. The salient features wore a resemblance. Prosperity and heartiness; a ready hand on, and over, a full purse; a recognised ability of the second-rate order; a stout hold of patent principles; inherited and embraced, to make the day secure and supply a somniferous pillow for the night; occasional fits of anxiety about affairs, followed by an illuminating conviction that the world is a changing one and our construction not of granite, nevertheless that a justifiable faith in the ship, joined to a constant study of the chart, will pull us through, as it has done before, despite all assaults and underminings of the common enemy and the particular; these, with the humorous indifference of familiarity and constitutional annoyances, excepting when they grew acute and called for drugs, and with friendliness to the race of man of both colours, in the belief that our Creator originally composed in black and white, together with a liking for matters on their present footing in slow motion, partly under his conductorship, were the prominent characteristics of the grandson of the founder of the house, who had built it from a spade.

The story of the building was notorious; popular books for the inciting of young Englishmen to dig to fortune had a place for it among the chapters, where we read of the kind of man, and the means by which the country has executed its later giant strides of advancement. The first John

Mattock was a representative of his time; he moved when the country was moving, and in the right direction, finding himself at the auspicious moment upon a line of rail. Elsewhere he would have moved, we may suppose, for the spade-like virtues bear their fruits; persistent and thrifty, solid and square, will fetch some sort of yield out of any soil; but he would not have gone far. The Lord, to whom an old man of a mind totally Hebrew ascribed the plenitude of material success, the Lord and he would have reared a garden in the desert; in proximity to an oasis, still on the sands, against obstacles. An accumulation of upwards of four hundred thousand pounds required, as the moral of the popular books does not sufficiently indicate, a moving country, an ardent sphere, to produce the sum: and since, where so much was done, we are bound to conceive others at work as well as he, it seems to follow that the exemplar outstripping them vastly must have profited by situation at the start, which is a lucky accident; and an accident is an indigestible lump in a moral tale, real though the story be. It was not mentioned in the popular books; nor did those worthy guides to the pursuit of wealth contain any reminder of old John Mattock's dependence upon the conjoint labour of his fellows to push him to his elevation. As little did they think of foretelling a day, generations hence, when the empty heirs of his fellows might prefer a modest claim (confused in statement) to compensation against the estate he bequeathed: for such prophecy as that would have hinted at a tenderness for the mass to the detriment of the individual, and such tenderness as that is an element of our religion, not the drift of our teaching.

He grumbled at the heavy taxation of his estate during life: yearly this oppressed old man paid thousands of pounds to the Government. It was poor encouragement to shoulder and elbow your way from a hovel to a mansion!

He paid the money, dying sour; a splendid example of energy on the road, a forbidding one at the terminus. And here the moral of the popular books turned aside from him to snatch at humanity for an instance of our frailness and dealt in portentous shadows:—we are, it should be known, not the great creatures we assume ourselves to be. Six months before his death he appeared in the garb of a navvy, humbly soliciting employment at his own house-door. There he appealed to the white calves of his footmen for a day's work, upon the plea that he had never been a democrat.

The scene had been described with humanely-moralising pathos in the various books of stories of Men who have come to Fortune, and it had for a length of seasons an annual position in the foremost rank (on the line, facing the door) in our exhibition of the chosen artists, where, as our popular words should do, it struck the spectator's eye and his brain simultaneously with pugilistic force: a reference to the picture in the catalogue furnishing a recapitulation of the incident. 'I've worked a good bit in my time, gentlemen, and I baint done yet':—SEE PROFESSOR SUMMIT'S 'MEN WHO HAVE COME TO FORTUNE.' There is, we perceive at a glance, a contrast in the bowed master of the Mansion applying to his menials for a day's work at the rate of pay to able-bodied men:—which he is not, but the deception is not disingenuous. The contrast flashed with the rapid exchange of two prizefighters in a ring, very popularly. The fustian suit and string below the knee, on the one side, and the purple plush breeches and twinkling airy calves (fascinating his attention as he makes his humble request to his own, these domestic knights) to right and left of the doorway and in front, hit straight out of the canvas. And as quickly as you perceive the contrast you swallow the moral. The dreaded thing is down in a trice, to do what salutary work it may within you. That it passed into the blood of England's middle-class population, and set many heads philosophically shaking, and filled the sails of many a sermon, is known to those who lived in days when Art and the classes patronising our Native Art existed happily upon the terms of venerable School-Dame and studious pupils, before the sickly era displacing Exhibitions full of meaning for tricks of colour, monstrous atmospherical vagaries that teach nothing, strange experiments on the complexion of the human face divine—the feminine hyper-aethereally. Like the first John Mattock, it was formerly of, and yet by dint of sturdy energy, above the people. They learnt from it; they flocked to it thirsting and retired from it thoughtful, with some belief of having drunk of nature in art, as you will see the countless troops of urchins about the one cow of London, in the Great City's Green Park.

A bequest to the nation of the best of these pictures of Old John, by a very old Yorkshire collector, makes it milk for all time, a perpetual contrast, and a rebuke. Compared with the portrait of Jane Mattock in her fiery aureole of hair on the walls of the breakfast-room, it marks that fatal period of degeneracy for us, which our critics of Literature as well as Art are one voice in denouncing, when the complex overwhelms the simple, and excess of signification is attempted, instead of letting plain nature speak her uncorrupted tongue to the contemplative mind. Degeneracy is the critical history of the Arts. Jane's hair was of a reddish gold-inwoven cast that would, in her grandfather's epoch, have shone unambiguously as carrots. The girl of his day thus adorned by Nature, would have been shown wearing her ridiculous crown with some decent sulkiness; and we should not have had her so unsparingly crowned; the truth would have been told in a dexterous concealment—a rope of it wound up for a bed of the tortoise-shell comb behind, and a pair of tight cornucopias at the temples. What does our modern artist do but flare it to right and left, lift it wavily over her forehead, revel in the oriental superabundance, and really seem to swear we shall admire it, against our traditions of the vegetable, as a poetical splendour. The head of the heiress is in a Jovian shower. Marigolds are in her hand. The whole square of canvas is like a meadow on the borders of June. It causes blinking.

Her brother also is presented: a fine portrait of him, with clipped red locks, in blue array, smiling, wearing the rose of briny breezes, a telescope under his left arm, his right forefinger on a map, a view of Spitzbergen through a cabin-window: for John had notions about the north-west passage, he had spent a winter in the ice, and if an amateur, was not the less a true sailor.

With his brass-buttoned blue coat, and his high coloured cheeks, and his convict hair—a layer of brickdust—and his air of princely wealth, and the icebergs and hummocks about him, he looks for adventure without a thought of his heroism—the country all over.

There he stands, a lover of the sea, and a scientific seaman and engineer to boot, practical in every line of his face, defying mankind to suspect that he cherishes a grain of romance. On the wall, just above his shoulder, is a sketch of a Viking putting the lighted brand to his ship in mid sea, and you are to understand that his time is come and so should a Viking die: further, if you will, the subject is a modern Viking, ready for the responsibilities of the title. Sketches of our ancient wooden walls and our iron and plated defences line the panellings. These degenerate artists do work hard for their money.

The portrait of John's father, dated a generation back, is just the man and little else, phantomly the man. His brown coat struggles out of the obscurity of the background, but it is chiefly background clothing him. His features are distinguishable and delicate: you would suppose him appearing to you under the beams of a common candle, or cottage coalfire—ferruginously opaque. The object of the artist (apart from the triumph of tone on the canvas) is to introduce him as an elegant and faded gentleman, rather retiring into darkness than emerging. He is the ghost of the painter's impasto. Yet this is Ezra Mattock, who multiplied the inheritance of the hundreds of thousands into millions, and died, after covering Europe, Asia, and the Americas with iron rails, one of the few Christians that can hold up their heads beside the banking Jew as magnates in the lists of gold. The portrait is clearly no frontispiece of his qualities. He married an accomplished and charitable lady, and she did not spoil the stock in refining it. His life passed quietly; his death shook the country: for though it had been known that he had been one of our potentates, how mightily he was one had not entered into the calculations of the public until the will of the late Ezra Mattock, cited in our prints, received comments from various newspaper articles. A chuckle of collateral satisfaction ran through the empire. All England and her dependencies felt the state of cousinship with the fruits of energy; and it was an agreeable sentiment, coming opportunely, as it did, at the tail of articles that had been discussing a curious manifestation of late—to-wit, the awakening energy of the foreigner—a prodigious apparition on our horizon. Others were energetic too! We were not, the sermon ran, to imagine we were without rivals in the field. We were possessed of certain positive advantages; we had coal, iron, and an industrious population, but we were, it was to be feared, by no means a thrifty race, and there was reason for doubt whether in the matter of industry we were quite up to the mark of our forefathers. No deterioration of the stock was apprehended, still the nation must be accused of a lack of vigilance. We must look round us, and accept the facts as they stood. So accustomed had we become to the predominance of our position that it was difficult at first to realise a position of rivalry that threatened our manufacturing interests in their hitherto undisputed lead in the world's markets. The tale of our exports for the last five years conveys at once its moral and its warning. Statistics were then cited.

As when the gloomy pedagogue has concluded his exhortation, statistics birched the land. They were started at our dinner-tables, and scourged the social converse. Not less than in the articles, they were perhaps livelier than in the preface; they were distressing nevertheless; they led invariably to the question of our decadence. Carthage was named; a great mercantile community absolutely obliterated! Senatorial men were led to propose in their thoughtfullest tones that we should turn our attention to Art. Why should we not learn to excel in Art? We excelled in Poetry. Our Poets were cited: not that there was a notion that poems would pay as an export but to show that if we excel in one of the Arts we may in others of them. The poetry was not cited, nor was it necessary, the object being to inflate the balloon of paradox with a light-flying gas, and prove a poem-producing people to be of their nature born artists; if they did but know it. The explosion of a particular trade points to your taking up another. Energy is adapted to flourish equally in every branch of labour.

It is the genius of the will, commanding all the crossroads. A country breeding hugely must prove its energy likewise in the departments of the mind, or it will ultimately be unable to feed its young—nay, to feast its aldermen! Let us be up and alive.—Such was the exhortation of a profound depression. Outside these dismal assemblies, in the streets, an ancient song of raven recurrence croaked of 'Old England a-going down the hill'; for there is a link of electricity between the street-boy and the leading article in days when the Poles exchange salutations.

Mr. Ezra's legacy of his millions to son and daughter broke like a golden evening on the borders of the raincloud. Things could not be so bad when a plain untitled English gentleman bequeathed in the simplest manner possible such giant heaps, a very Pelion upon Ossa, of wealth to his children. The minds of the readers of journals were now directed to think of the hoarded treasures of this favoured country. They might approximately be counted, but even if counted they would be past conception, like the sidereal system. The contemplation of a million stupefies: consider the figures of millions and millions! Articles were written on Lombard Street, the world's gold-mine, our granary of energy, surpassing all actual and fabulous gold-mines ever spoken of: Aladdin's magician would find his purse contracting and squeaking in the comparison. Then, too, the store of jewels held by certain private families called for remark and an allusion to Sindbad the sailor, whose eyes were to dilate wider than they did in the valley of diamonds. Why, we could, if we pleased, lie by and pass two or three decades as jolly cricketers and scullers, and resume the race for wealth with the rest of mankind, hardly sensible of the holiday in our pockets though we were the last people to do it, we were the sole people that had the option. Our Fortunatus' cap was put to better purposes, but to have the cap, and not to be emasculated by the possession, might excuse a little reasonable pride in ourselves.

Thus did Optimism and Pessimism have their turn, like the two great parties in the State, and the subsiding see-saw restored a proper balance, much to the nation's comfort. Unhappily, it was remembered, there are spectators of its method of getting to an equipoise out of the agitation of extremes. The peep at our treasures to regain composure had, we fear, given the foreigner glimpses, and whetted the appetite of our masses. No sooner are we at peace than these are heard uttering low howls, and those are seen enviously glaring. The spectre, Panic, that ever dogs the optimistic feast, warns us of a sack under our beds, and robbers about to try a barely-bolted door... Then do we, who have so sweetly sung our senses to sleep, start up, in their grip, rush to the doctor and the blacksmith, rig alarums, proclaim ourselves intestinally torn, defenceless, a prey to foes within and without. It is discovered to be no worse than an alderman's dream, but the pessimist frenzy of the night has tossed a quieting sop to the Radical, and summoned the volunteers to a review. Laudatory articles upon the soldierly 'march past' of our volunteers permit of a spell of soft repose, deeper than prudent, at the end of it, India and Ireland consenting.

So much for a passing outline of John Bull—the shadow on the wall of John Mattock. The unostentatious millionaire's legacy to his two children affected Mr. Bull thrillingly, pretty nearly as it has here been dotted in lining. That is historical. Could he believe in the existence of a son of his, a master of millions, who had never sighed (and he had only to sigh) to die a peer, or a baronet, or simple Knight? The downright hard-nailed coffin fact was there; the wealthiest man in the country had flown away to Shadowland a common Mr.! You see the straight deduction from the circumstances:—we are, say what you will, a Republican people! Newspaper articles on the watch sympathetically for Mr. Bull's latest view of himself, preached on the theme of our peculiar Republicanism. Soon after he was observed fondling the Crown Insignia. His bards flung out their breezy columns, reverentially monarchial. The Republican was informed that they were despised as a blatant minority. A maudlin fit of worship of our nobility had hold of him next, and English aristocracy received the paean. Lectures were addressed to democrats; our House of Lords was pledged solemnly in reams of print. We were told that 'blood' may always be betted on to win the race; blood that is blue will beat the red hollow. Who could pretend to despise the honour of admission to the ranks of the proudest peerage the world has known! Is not a great territorial aristocracy the strongest guarantee of national stability? The loudness of the interrogation, like the thunder of Jove, precluded thought of an answer.

Mr. Bull, though he is not of lucid memory, kept an eye on the owner of those millions. His bards were awake to his anxiety, and celebrated John Mattock's doings with a trump and flourish somewhat displeasing to a quietly-disposed commoner. John's entry into Parliament as a Liberal was taken for a sign of steersman who knew where the tide ran. But your Liberals are sometimes Radicals in their youth, and his choice of parties might not be so much sagacity as an instance of unripe lightheadedness. A young conservative millionaire is less disturbing. The very wealthy young peer is never wanton in his politics, which seems to admonish us that the heir of vast wealth should have it imposed on him to accept a peerage, and be locked up as it were. A coronet steadies the brain. You may let out your heels at the social laws, you are almost expected to do it, but you are to shake that young pate of yours restively under such a splendid encumbrance. Private reports of John, however, gave him credit for sound opinions: he was moderate, merely progressive. When it was added that the man had the habit of taking counsel with his sister, he was at once considered as fast and safe, not because of any public knowledge of the character of Jane Mattock. We pay this homage to the settled common sense of women. Distinctly does she discountenance leaps in the dark, wild driving, and the freaks of Radicalism.

John, as it happened, had not so grave a respect for the sex as for the individual Jane. He thought women capable of acts of foolishness; his bright-faced sister he could thoroughly trust for prudent conduct. He gave her a good portion of his heart in confidence, and all of it in affection. There were matters which he excluded from confidence, even from intimate communication with himself. These he could not reveal; nor could she perfectly open her heart to him, for the same reason. They both had an established ideal of their personal qualities, not far above the positive, since they were neither of them pretentious, yet it was a trifle higher and fairer than the working pattern; and albeit they were sincere enough, quite sincere in their mutual intercourse, they had, by what each knew at times of the thumping organ within them, cause for doubting that they were as transparent as the other supposed; and they were separately aware of an inward smile at one another's partial deception; which did not thwart their honest power of working up to the respected ideal. The stroke of the deeper self-knowledge rarely shook them; they were able to live with full sensations in the animated picture they were to the eyes best loved by them. This in fact was their life. Anything beside it was a dream, and we do not speak of our dreams—not of every dream. Especially do we reserve our speech concerning the dream in which we had a revelation of the proud frame deprived of a guiding will, flung rudderless on the waves. Ah that abject! The dismantled ship has the grandeur of the tempest about it, but the soul swayed by passion is ignominiously bare-poled, detected, hooted by its old assumption. If instinct plays fantastical tricks when we are sleeping, let it be ever behind a curtain. We can be held guilty only if we court exposure. The ideal of English gentleman and gentlewoman is closely Roman in the self-repression it exacts, and that it should be but occasionally difficult to them shows an affinity with the type. Do you perchance, O continental observers of the race, call it hypocritical? It is their nature disciplined to the regimental step of civilisation. Socially these island men and women of a certain middle rank are veterans of an army, and some of the latest enrolled are the stoutest defenders of the flag.

    Brother and sister preserved their little secrets of character apart. They could not be expected to unfold what they declined personally to examine. But they were not so successful with the lady governing the household, their widowed maternal aunt, Mrs. Lackstraw, a woman of decisive penetration, and an insubordinate recruit of the army aforesaid. To her they were without a mask; John was passion's slave, Jane the most romantic of Eve's daughters. She pointed to incidents of their youth; her vision was acutely retrospective. The wealth of her nephew and niece caused such a view of them to be, as she remarked, anxious past endurance. She had grounds for fearing that John, who might step to an alliance with any one of the proudest houses in the Kingdom, would marry a beggar-maid. As for Jane, she was the natural prey of a threadbare poet. Mrs. Lackstraw heard of Mr. Patrick O'Donnell, and demanded the right to inspect him. She doubted such perfect disinterestedness in any young man as that he should slave at account-keeping to that Laundry without a prospect of rich remuneration, and the tale of his going down to the city for a couple of hours each day to learn the art of keeping books was of very dubious import in a cousin of Captain Con O'Donnell. 'Let me see your prodigy,' she said, with the emphasis on each word. Patrick was presented at her table. She had steeled herself against an Irish tongue. He spoke little, appeared simple, professed no enthusiasm for the Laundry. And he paid no compliments to Jane: of the two he was more interested by the elder lady, whose farm and dairy in Surrey he heard her tell of with a shining glance, observing that he liked thick cream: there was a touch of home in it. The innocent sensuality in the candid avowal of his tastes inspired confidence. Mrs. Lackstraw fished for some account of his home. He was open to flow on the subject; he dashed a few sketches of mother and sisters, dowerless girls, fresh as trout in the stream, and of his own poor estate, and the peasantry, with whom he was on friendly terms. He was an absentee for his education. Sweet water, pure milk, potatoes and bread, were the things he coveted in plenty for his people and himself, he said, calling forth an echo from Mrs. Lackstraw, and an invitation to come down to her farm in the Spring. 'That is, Mr. O'Donnell, if you are still in London.'

'Oh, I'm bound apprentice for a year,' said he.

He was asked whether he did not find it tiresome work.

'A trifle so,' he confessed.

Then why did he pursue it, the question was put.

He was not alive for his own pleasure, and would like to feel he was doing a bit of good, was the answer.

Could one, Mrs. Lackstraw asked herself, have faith in this young Irishman? He possessed an estate. His brogue rather added to his air of truthfulness. His easy manners and the occasional streak of correct French in his dialogue cast a shadow on it. Yet he might be an ingenuous creature precisely because of the suspicion roused by his quaint unworldliness that he might be a terrible actor. Why not?—his heart was evidently much more interested in her pursuits than in her niece's. The juvenility of him was catching, if it was indeed the man, and not one of the actor's properties. Mrs. Lackstraw thought it prudent to hint at the latter idea to Jane while she decided in her generosity to embrace the former. Oh! if all Irishmen shared his taste for sweet water, pure milk and wholesome bread, what a true Union we should have! She had always insisted on those three things as most to be desired on earth for the masses, and she reminded Jane of it as a curious fact. Jane acquiesced, having always considered it a curious fact that her aunt should combine the relish of a country life with the intensest social ambition—a passion so sensitive as to make the name her husband had inflicted on her a pain and a burden. The name of Mattock gave her horrors. She spoke of it openly to prove that Jane must marry a title and John become a peer. Never was there such a name to smell of the soil. She declared her incapacity to die happy until the two had buried Mattock. Her own one fatal step condemned her, owing to the opinion she held upon the sacredness of marriage, as Lackstraw on her tombstone, and to Lackstraw above the earthly martyr would go bearing the designation which marked her to be claimed by him. But for John and Jane the index of Providence pointed a brighter passage through life. They had only to conquer the weakness native to them—the dreadful tendency downward. They had, in the spiritual sense, frail hearts. The girl had been secretive about the early activity of hers, though her aunt knew of two or three adventures wanting in nothing save boldness to have put an end to her independence and her prospects:—hence this Laundry business! a clear sign of some internal disappointment. The boy, however, had betrayed himself in his mother's days, when it required all her influence and his father's authority, with proof positive of the woman's unworthiness, to rescue him from immediate disaster.

Mrs. Lackstraw's confidences on the theme of the family she watched over were extended to Patrick during their strolls among the ducks and fowls and pheasants at her farm. She dealt them out in exclamations, as much as telling him that now they knew him they trusted him, notwithstanding the unaccountable part he played as honorary secretary to that Laundry. The confidences, he was aware, were common property of the visitors one after another, but he had the knowledge of his being trusted as not every Irishman would have been. A service of six months to the secretaryship established his reputation as the strange bird of a queer species: not much less quiet, honest, methodical, than an Englishman, and still impulsive, Irish still; a very strange bird.

The disposition of the English to love the children of Erin, when not fretted by them, was shown in the treatment Patrick received from the Mattock family. It is a love resembling the affection of the stage-box for a set of favourite performers, and Patrick, a Celt who had schooled his wits to observe and meditate, understood his position with them as one of the gallant and amusing race, as well as the reason why he had won their private esteem. They are not willingly suspicious: it agitates their minds to be so; and they are most easily lulled by the flattery of seeing their special virtues grafted on an alien stock: for in this admiration of virtues that are so necessary to the stalwart growth of man, they become just sensible of a minor deficiency; the tree, if we jump out of it to examine its appearance, should not be all trunk. Six months of ungrudging unremunerated service, showing devotion to the good cause and perfect candour from first to last, was English, and a poetic touch beyond: so that John Mattock, if he had finished the sentence instead of lopping it with an interjection, would have said: 'These Irish fellows, when they're genuine and first rate!—are pretty well the pick of the land.' Perhaps his pause on the interjection expressed a doubt of our getting them genuine. Mr. O'Donnell was a sort of exceptional Irishman, not devoid of practical ability in a small way—he did his duties of secretary fairly well; apparently sincere—he had refrained from courting Jane; an odd creature enough, what with his mixture of impulsiveness and discretion; likeable, pleasant to entertain and talk to; not one of your lunatics concerning his country—he could listen to an Englishman's opinion on that head, listen composedly to Rockney, merely seeming to take notes; and Rockney was, as Captain Con termed him, Press Dragoon about Ireland, a trying doctor for a child of the patient.

On the whole, John Mattock could shake his hand heartily when he was leaving our shores. Patrick was released by Miss Grace Barrow's discovery at last of a lady capable of filling his place: a circumstance that he did not pretend to regret. He relinquished his post and stood aside with the air of a disciplined soldier. This was at the expiration of seven months and two weeks of service. Only after he had gone, upon her receiving his first letter from the Continent, did Jane distinguish in herself the warmth of friendliness she felt for him, and know that of all around her she, reproaching every one who had hinted a doubt, had been the most suspicious of his pure simplicity. It was the vice of her condition to be suspicious of the honesty of men. She thought of her looks as less attractive than they were; of her wealth she had reason to think that the scent transformed our sad sex into dogs under various disguises. Remembering her chill once on hearing Patrick in a green lane where they botanised among spring flowers call himself her Irish cousin, as if he had advanced a step and betrayed the hoof, she called him her Irish cousin now in good earnest. Her nation was retrospectively enthusiastic. The cordiality of her letter of reply to the wandering Patrick astonished him on the part of so cool a young lady; and Captain Con, when he heard Miss Mattock speak of Patrick to his wife, came to the conclusion that the leery lad had gone a far way toward doing the trick for himself, though Jane said his correspondence was full of the deeds of his brother in India. She quite sparkled in speaking of this boy.

She and the captain had an interchange of sparklings over absent Patrick, at a discovery made by Miss Colesworth, the lady replacing him, in a nook of the amateur secretary's official desk, under heaps of pamphlets and slips, French and English and Irish journals, not at all bearing upon the business of the Laundry. It was a blotting-pad stuffed with Patrick's jottings. Jane brought it to Con as to the proper keeper of the reliquary. He persuaded her to join him in examining it, and together they bent their heads, turning leaf by leaf, facing, laughing, pursuing the search for more, sometimes freely shouting.

Her inspection of the contents had previously been shy; she had just enough to tell her they were funny. Dozens of scraps, insides of torn envelopes, invitation-cards, ends of bills received from home, whatever was handy to him at the moment, had done service for the overflow of Mr. Secretary's private notes and reflections; the blotting-paper as well; though that was devoted chiefly to sketches of the human countenance, the same being almost entirely of the fair. Jane fancied she spied herself among the number. Con saw the likeness, but not considering it a complimentary one, he whisked over the leaf. Grace Barrow was unmistakeable. Her dimpled cushion features, and very intent eyes gazing out of the knolls and dingles, were given without caricature. Miss Colesworth appeared on the last page, a half-length holding a big key, demure between curls. The key was explained by a cage on a stool, and a bird flying out. She had unlocked the cage for Patrick.

'He never seemed anxious to be released while he was at work,' said Jane, after she and the captain had spelt the symbolling in turns.

'And never thirsted to fly till he flew, I warrant him,' said Con.

A repeated sketch of some beauty confused them both; neither of them could guess the proud owner of those lineaments. Con proclaimed it to be merely one of the lad's recollections, perhaps a French face. He thought he might have seen a face rather resembling it, but could not call to mind whose face it was.

'I dare say it's just a youngster's dream on a stool at a desk, as poets write sonnets in their youth to nobody, till they're pierced by somebody, and then there's a difference in their handwriting,' he said, vexed with Patrick for squandering his opportunity to leave a compliment to the heiress behind him.

Jane flipped the leaves back to the lady with stormy hair.

'But you'll have the whole book, and hand it to him when he returns; it'll come best from you,' said Con. 'The man on horseback, out of uniform, 's brother Philip, of course. And man and horse are done to the life. Pray, take it, Miss Mattock. I should lose it to a certainty; I should; I can't be trusted. You'll take it!'

He pressed her so warmly to retain the bundle in her custody that she carried it away.

Strange to say the things she had laughed at had been the things which struck her feelings and sympathies. Patrick's notes here and there recalled conversations he had more listened to than taken part in between herself and Grace Barrow. Who could help laughing at his ideas about women! But if they were crude, they were shrewd—or so she thought them; and the jejuneness was, to her mind, chiefly in the dressing of them. Grace agreed with her, for Grace had as good a right to inspect the papers as she, and a glance had shown that there was nothing of peculiar personal import in his notes: he did not brood on himself.

Here was one which tickled the ladies and formed a text for discussion.

'Women must take the fate of market-fruit till they earn their own pennies, and then they 'll regulate the market. It is a tussle for money with them as with us, meaning power. They'd do it as little by oratory as they have done by millinery, for their oratory, just like their millinery, appeals to a sentiment, and to a weaker; and nothing solid comes of a sentiment. Power is built on work.'

To this was appended: 'The better for mankind in the developing process, ay, and a bad day for us, boys, when study masks the charming eyes in gig-lamps, and there is no pretty flying before us. Good-night to Cupid, I fear. May be I am not seeing far enough, and am asking for the devil to have the loveliest women as of old. Retro S. M.'

The youthful eye on their sex, the Irish voice, and the perceptible moral earnestness in the background, made up a quaint mixture.

CHAPTER XVI. OF THE GREAT MR. BULL AND THE CELTIC AND SAXON VIEW OF HIM: AND SOMETHING OF RICHARD ROCKNEY

Meanwhile India, our lubber giant, had ceased to kick a leg, and Ireland, our fever-invalid, wore the aspect of an opiate slumber. The volcano we couch on was quiet, the gritty morsel unabsorbed within us at an armistice with the gastric juices. Once more the personification of the country's prosperity had returned to the humming state of roundness. Trade whipped him merrily, and he spun.

A fuller sketch of the figure of this remarkable emanation of us and object of our worship, Bull, is required that we may breathe the atmosphere of a story dealing with such very different views of the idol, and learn to tolerate plain-speaking about him.

Fancy yourself delayed by stress of weather at an inn or an excursion, and snapped up by some gossip drone of the district, who hearing whither you are bound, recounts the history and nature of the place, to your ultimate advantage, though you groan for the outer downpour to abate.—Of Bull, then: our image, before the world: our lord and tyrant, ourself in short—the lower part of us. Coldly worshipped on the whole, he can create an enthusiasm when his roast-beef influence mounts up to peaceful skies and the domestic English world spins with him. What he does not like will then be the forbidding law of a most governable people, what he does like the consenting. If it is declared that argument will be inefficacious to move him, he is adored in the form of post. A hint of his willingness in any direction, causes a perilous rush of his devotees. Nor is there reason to suppose we have drawn the fanatical subserviency from the example of our subject India. We may deem it native; perhaps of its origin Aryan, but we have made it our own. Some have been so venturesome as to trace the lordliness of Bull to the protecting smiles of the good Neptune, whose arms are about him to encourage the development of a wanton eccentricity. Certain weeds of the human bosom are prompt to flourish where safeness would seem to be guaranteed. Men, for instance, of stoutly independent incomes are prone to the same sort of wilfulness as Bull's, the salve abject submission to it which we behold in his tidal bodies of supporters. Neptune has done something. One thinks he has done much, at a rumour of his inefficiency to do the utmost. Spy you insecurity?—a possibility of invasion? Then indeed the colossal creature, inaccessible to every argument, is open to any suggestion: the oak-like is a reed, the bull a deer. But as there is no attack on his shores, there is no proof that they are invulnerable. Neptune is appealed to and replies by mouth of the latest passenger across the Channel on a windy night:—Take heart, son John! They will have poor stomachs for blows who intrude upon you. The testification to the Sea-God's watchfulness restores his darling who is immediately as horny to argument as before. Neptune shall have his share of the honours.

Ideal of his country Bull has none—he hates the word; it smells of heresy, opposition to his image. It is an exercise of imagination to accept an ideal, and his digestive organs reject it, after the manner of the most beautiful likeness of him conjurable to the mind—that flowering stomach, the sea-anemone, which opens to anything and speedily casts out what it cannot consume. He is a positive shape, a practical corporation, and the best he can see is the mirror held up to him by his bards of the Press and his jester Frank Guffaw. There, begirt by laughing ocean-waves, manifestly blest, he glorifies his handsome roundness, like that other Foam-Born, whom the decorative Graces robed in vestments not so wonderful as printed sheets. Rounder at each inspection, he preaches to mankind from the text of a finger curved upon the pattern spectacles. Your Frenchmen are revolutionising, wagering on tentative politics; your Germans ploughing in philosophy, thumbing classics, composing music of a novel order: both are marching, evolutionising, learning how to kill. Ridiculous Germans! capricious Frenchmen! We want nothing new in musical composition and abstract speculation of an indecent mythology, or political contrivances and schemes of Government, and we do not want war. Peace is the Goddess we court for the hand of her daughter Plenty, and we have won that jolly girl, and you are welcome to the marriage-feast; but avaunt new-fangled theories and howlings: old tunes, tried systems, for us, my worthy friends.

Roundness admiring the growth of its globe may address majestic invitation to the leaner kine. It can exhibit to the world that Peace is a most desirable mother-in-law; and it is tempted to dream of capping the pinnacle of wisdom when it squats on a fundamental truth. Bull's perusal of the Horatian carpe diem is acute as that of the cattle in fat meads; he walks like lusty Autumn carrying his garner to drum on, for a sign of his diligent wisdom in seizing the day. He can read the page fronting him; and let it be of dining, drinking, toasting, he will vociferously confute the wiseacre bookworms who would have us believe there is no such thing as a present hour for man.

In sad fact, the member for England is often intoxicate. Often do we have him whirling his rotundity like a Mussulman dervish inflated by the spirit to agitate the shanks, until pangs of a commercial crisis awaken him to perceive an infructuous past and an unsown future, without one bit of tracery on its black breast other than that which his apprehensions project. As for a present hour, it swims, it vanishes, thinner than the phantom banquets of recollection. What has he done for the growth of his globe of brains?—the lesser, but in our rightful posture the upper, and justly the directing globe, through whose directions we do, by feeding on the past to sow the future, create a sensible present composed of both—the present of the good using of our powers. What can he show in the Arts? What in Arms? His bards—O faithless! but they are men—his bards accuse him of sheer cattle-contentedness in the mead, of sterility of brain, drowsihood, mid-noddyism, downright carcase-dulness. They question him to deafen him of our defences, our intellectual eminence, our material achievements, our poetry, our science; they sneer at his trust in Neptune, doubt the scaly invulnerability of the God. They point over to the foreigner, the clean-stepping, braced, self-confident foreigner, good at arms, good at the arts, and eclipsing us in industriousness manual and mental, and some dare to say, in splendour of verse=-our supreme accomplishment.

Then with one big fellow, the collapse of pursiness, he abandons his pedestal of universal critic; prostrate he falls to the foreigner; he is down, he is roaring; he is washing his hands of English performances, lends ear to foreign airs, patronises foreign actors, browses on reports from camps of foreign armies. He drops his head like a smitten ox to all great foreign names, moaning 'Shakespeare!' internally for a sustaining apostrophe. He well-nigh loves his poets, can almost understand what poetry means. If it does not pay, it brings him fame, respectfulness in times of reverse. Brains, he is reduced to apprehend, brains are the generators of the conquering energies. He is now for brains at all costs, he has gained a conception of them. He is ready to knock knighthood on the heads of men of brains—even literary brains. They shall be knights, an ornamental body. To make them peers, and a legislative, has not struck him, for he has not yet imagined them a stable body. They require petting, to persuade them to flourish and bring him esteem.

This is Mr. Bull, our image before the world, whose pranks are passed as though the vivid display of them had no bad effect on the nation. Doubtless the perpetual mirror, the slavish mirror, is to blame, but his nakedness does not shrink from the mirror, he likes it and he is proud of it. Beneath these exhibitions the sober strong spirit of the country, unfortunately not a prescient one, nor an attractively loveable, albeit of a righteous benevolence, labours on, doing the hourly duties for the sake of conscience, little for prospective security, little to win affection. Behold it as the donkey of a tipsy costermonger, obedient to go without the gift of expression. Its behaviour is honourable under a discerning heaven, and there is ever something pathetic in a toilful speechlessness; but it is of dogged attitude in the face of men. Salt is in it to keep our fleshly grass from putrefaction; poets might proclaim its virtues. They will not; they are averse. The only voice it has is the Puritan bray, upon which one must philosophise asinically to unveil the charm. So the world is pleased to let it be obscured by the paunch of Bull. We have, however, isolated groups, individuals in all classes, by no means delighting in his representation of them. When such is felt to be the case among a sufficient number, his bards blow him away as a vapour; we hear that he is a piece of our English humour—we enjoy grotesques and never should agree to paint ourselves handsome: our subtle conceit insists on the reverse. Nevertheless, no sooner are the hours auspicious to fatness than Bull is back on us; he is our family goat, ancestral ghost, the genius of our comfortable sluggishness. And he is at times a mad Bull: a foaming, lashing, trampling, horn-driving, excessive, very parlous Bull. It is in his history that frenzies catch him, when to be yoked to him is to suffer frightful shakings, not to mention a shattering of our timbers. It is but in days of the rousing of the under-spirit of the country, days of storm imprudent to pray the advent of, that we are well rid of him for a while. In the interim he does mischief, serious mischief; he does worse than when, a juvenile, he paid the Dannegelt for peace. Englishmen of feeling do not relish him. For men with Irish and Cambrian blood in their veins the rubicund grotesque, with his unimpressionable front and his noisy benevolence of the pocket, his fits of horned ferocity and lapses of hardheartedness, is a shame and a loathing. You attach small importance to images and symbols; yet if they seem representative, and they sicken numbers of us, they are important. The hat we wear, though it is not a part of the head, stamps the character of our appearance and has a positive influence on our bearing. Symbolical decorations will stimulate the vacant-minded to act up to them, they encircle and solidify the mass; they are a sword of division between Celts and Saxons if they are abhorrent to one section. And the Celtic brotherhood are not invariably fools in their sensitiveness. They serve you on the field of Mars, and on other fields to which the world has given glory. These execrate him as the full-grown Golden Calf of heathenish worship. And they are so restive because they are so patriotic. Think a little upon the ideas of unpatriotic Celts regarding him. You have heard them. You tell us they are you: accurately, they affirm, succinctly they see you in his crescent outlines, tame bulk, spasms of alarm and foot on the weaker; his imperviousness to whatsoever does not confront the sensual eye of him with a cake or a fist, his religious veneration of his habitual indulgences, his peculiar forms of nightmare. They swear to his perfect personification of your moods, your Saxon moods, which their inconsiderate spleen would have us take for unmixedly Saxon. They are unjust, but many of them speak with a sense of the foot on their necks, and they are of a blood demanding a worshipworthy idea. And they dislike Bull's bellow of disrespect for their religion, much bruited in the meadows during his periods of Arcadia. They dislike it, cannot forget the sound: it hangs on the afflicted drum of the ear when they are in another land, perhaps when the old devotion to their priest has expired. For this, as well as for material reasons, they hug the hatred they packed up among their bundles of necessaries and relics, in the flight from home, and they instruct their children to keep it burning. They transmit the sentiment of the loathing of Bull, as assuredly they would be incapable of doing, even with the will, were a splendid fire-eyed motherly Britannia the figure sitting in the minds of men for our image—a palpitating figure, alive to change, penetrable to thought, and not a stolid concrete of our traditional old yeoman characteristic. Verily he lives for the present, all for the present, will be taught in sorrow that there is no life for him but of past and future: his delusion of the existence of a present hour for man will not outlast the season of his eating and drinking abundantly in security. He will perceive that it was no more than the spark shot out from the clash of those two meeting forces; and penitently will he gaze back on that misleading spark-the spectral planet it bids wink to his unreceptive stars—acknowledging him the bare machine for those two to drive, no instrument of enjoyment. He lives by reading rearward and seeing vanward. He has no actual life save in power of imagination. He has to learn this fact, the great lesson of all men. Furthermore there may be a future closed to him if he has thrown too extreme a task of repairing on that bare machine of his. The sight of a broken-down plough is mournful, but the one thing to do with it is to remove it from the field.

 Among the patriotic of stout English substance, who blew in the trumpet of the country, and were not bards of Bull to celebrate his firmness and vindicate his shiftings, Richard Rockney takes front rank. A journalist altogether given up to his craft, considering the audience he had gained, he was a man of forethought besides being a trenchant writer, and he was profoundly, not less than eminently, the lover of Great Britain. He had a manner of utterance quite in the tone of the familiar of the antechamber for proof of his knowing himself to be this person. He did not so much write articles upon the health of his mistress as deliver Orphic sentences. He was in one her physician, her spiritual director, her man-at-arms. Public allusions to her were greeted with his emphatic assent in a measured pitch of the voice, or an instantaneous flourish of the rapier; and the flourish was no vain show. He meant hard steel to defend the pill he had prescribed for her constitutional state, and the monition for her soul's welfare. Nor did he pretend to special privileges in assuming his militant stand, but simply that he had studied her case, was intimate with her resources, and loved her hotly, not to say inspiredly. Love her as well, you had his cordial hand; as wisely, then all his weapons to back you. There were occasions when distinguished officials and Parliamentary speakers received the impetus of Rockney's approval and not hesitatingly he stepped behind them to bestow it. The act, in whatever fashion it may have been esteemed by the objects propelled, was a sign of his willingness to let the shadow of any man adopting his course obscure him, and of the simplicity of his attachment. If a bitter experience showed that frequently, indeed generally, they travelled scarce a tottering stagger farther than they were precipitated, the wretched consolation afforded by a side glance at a more enlightened passion, solitary in its depth, was Rockney's. Others perchance might equal his love, none the wisdom of it; actually none the vigilant circumspection, the shaping forethought. That clear knowledge of the right thing for the country was grasped but by fits by others. Enough to profit them this way and yonder as one best can! You know the newspaper Press is a mighty engine. Still he had no delight in shuffling a puppetry; he would have preferred automatic figures. His calls for them resounded through the wilderness of the wooden.

Any solid conviction of a capable head of a certainty impressed upon the world, and thus his changes of view were not attributed to a fluctuating devotion; they passed out of the range of criticism upon inconsistency, notwithstanding that the commencement of his journalistic career smelt of sources entirely opposed to the conclusions upon which it broadened. One secret of the belief in his love of his country was the readiness of Rockney's pen to support our nobler patriotic impulses, his relish of the bluff besides. His eye was on our commerce, on our courts of Law, on our streets and alleys, our army and navy, our colonies, the vaster than the island England, and still he would be busy picking up needles and threads in the island. Deeds of valour were noted by him, lapses of cowardice: how one man stood against a host for law or humanity, how crowds looked on at the beating of a woman, how a good fight was maintained in some sly ring between two of equal brawn: and manufacturers were warned of the consequences of their iniquities, Government was lashed for sleeping upon shaky ordinances, colonists were gibbeted for the maltreating of natives: the ring and fervour of the notes on daily events told of Rockney's hand upon the national heart—with a faint, an enforced, reluctant indication of our not being the men we were.

But after all, the main secret was his art of writing round English, instead of laborious Latinised periods: and the secret of the art was his meaning what he said. It was the personal throb. The fire of a mind was translucent in Press columns where our public had been accustomed to the rhetoric of primed scribes. He did away with the Biscay billow of the leading article—Bull's favourite prose—bardic construction of sentences that roll to the antithetical climax, whose foamy top is offered and gulped as equivalent to an idea. Writing of such a kind as Rockney's was new to a land where the political opinions of Joint Stock Companies had rattled Jovian thunders obedient to the nod of Bull. Though not alone in working the change, he was the foremost. And he was not devoid of style. Fervidness is the core of style. He was a tough opponent for his betters in education, struck forcibly, dexterously, was always alert for debate.

An encounter between Swift and Johnson, were it imaginable, would present us probably the most prodigious Gigantomachy in literary polemics. It is not imaginable among comparative pygmies. But Rockney's combat with his fellow-politicians of the Press partook of the Swiftian against the Johnsonian in form. He was a steam ram that drove straight at the bulky broadside of the enemy.

Premiers of parties might be Captains of the State for Rockney: Rockney was the premier's pilot, or woe to him. Woe to the country as well, if Rockney's directions for steering were unheeded. He was a man of forethought, the lover of Great Britain: he shouted his directions in the voice of the lover of his mistress, urged to rebuke, sometimes to command, the captain by the prophetic intimations of a holier alliance, a more illumined prescience. Reefs here, shallows there, yonder a foul course: this is the way for you! The refusal of the captain to go this way caused Rockney sincerely to discredit the sobriety of his intellect. It was a drunken captain. Or how if a traitorous? We point out the danger to him, and if he will run the country on to it, we proclaim him guilty either of inebriety or of treason—the alternatives are named: one or the other has him. Simple unfitness can scarcely be conceived of a captain having our common senses and a warranted pilot at his elbow.

Had not Rockney been given to a high expression of opinion, plain in fervour, he would often have been exposed bare to hostile shafts. Style cast her aegis over him. He wore an armour in which he could walk, run and leap-a natural style. The ardour of his temperament suffused the directness of his intelligence to produce it, and the two qualities made his weakness and strength. Feeling the nerve of strength, the weakness was masked to him, while his opponents were equally insensible to the weakness under the force of his blows. Thus there was nothing to teach him, or reveal him, except Time, whose trick is to turn corners of unanticipated sharpness, and leave the directly seeing and ardent to dash at walls.

How rigidly should the man of forethought govern himself, question himself! how constantly wrestle with himself! And if he be a writer ebullient by the hour, how snappishly suspect himself, that he may feel in conscience worthy of a hearing and have perpetually a conscience in his charge! For on what is his forethought founded? Does he try the ring of it with our changed conditions? Bus a man of forethought who has to be one of our geysers ebullient by the hour must live days of fever. His apprehensions distemper his blood; the scrawl of them on the dark of the undeveloped dazzles his brain. He sees in time little else; his very sincereness twists him awry. Such a man has the stuff of the born journalist, and journalism is the food of the age. Ask him, however, midway in his running, what he thinks of quick breathing: he will answer that to be a shepherd on the downs is to be more a man. As to the gobbling age, it really thinks better of him than he of it.

After a term of prolonged preachification he is compelled to lash that he may less despise the age. He has to do it for his own sake. O gobbling age! swallowing all, digesting nought, us too you have swallowed, O insensate mechanism! and we will let you know you have a stomach. Furiously we disagree with you. We are in you to lead you or work you pangs!

Rockney could not be a mild sermoniser commenting on events. Rather no journalism at all for him! He thought the office of the ordinary daily preacher cowlike. His gadfly stung him to warn, dictate, prognosticate; he was the oracle and martyr of superior vision: and as in affairs of business and the weighing of men he was of singularly cool sagacity, hard on the downright, open to the humours of the distinct discrimination of things in their roughness, the knowledge of the firmly-based materialism of his nature caused him thoroughly to trust to his voice when he delivered it in ardour—circumstance coming to be of daily recurrence. Great love creates forethoughtfulness, without which incessant journalism is a gabble. He was sure of his love, but who gave ear to his prescience? Few: the echo of the country now and then, the Government not often. And, dear me! those jog-trot sermonisers, mere commentators upon events, manage somehow to keep up the sale of their journals: advertisements do not flow and ebb with them as under the influence of a capricious moon. Ah, what a public! Serve it honourably, you are in peril of collapsing: show it nothing but the likeness of its dull animal face, you are steadily inflated. These reflections within us! Might not one almost say that the retreat for the prophet is the wilderness, far from the hustled editor's desk; and annual should be the uplifting of his voice instead of diurnal, if only to spare his blood the distemper? A fund of gout was in Rockney's, and he had begun to churn it. Between gouty blood and luminous brain the strife had set in which does not conduce to unwavering sobriety of mind, though ideas remain closely consecutive and the utterance resonant.

Never had he been an adulator of Bull. His defects as well as his advantages as a politician preserved to him this virtue. Insisting on a future, he could not do homage to the belying simulacrum of the present. In the season of prosperity Rockney lashed the old fellow with the crisis he was breeding for us; and when prostration ensued no English tongue was loftier in preaching dignity and the means of recovery. Our monumental image of the Misuse of Peace he pointed out unceasingly as at a despot constructed by freemen out of the meanest in their natures to mock the gift of liberty. His articles of foregone years were an extraordinary record of events or conditions foreseen: seductive in the review of them by a writer who has to be still foreseeing: nevertheless, that none of them were bardic of Bull, and that our sound man would have acted wisely in heeding some of the prescriptions, constituted their essential merit, consolatory to think of, though painful. The country has gone the wrong road, but it may yet cross over to the right one, when it perceives that we were prophetic.

Compared with the bolts discharged at Bull by Rockney's artillery, Captain Con O'Donnell's were popgun-pellets. Only Rockney fired to chasten, Con O'Donnell for a diversion, to appease an animus. The revolutionist in English journalism was too devoutly patriotic to belabour even a pantomime mask that was taken as representative of us for the disdainful fun of it. Behind the plethoric lamp, now blown with the fleshpots, now gasping puffs of panic, he saw the well-minded valorous people, issue of glorious grandsires; a nation under a monstrous defacement, stupefied by the contemplation of the mask: his vision was of the great of old, the possibly great in the graver strife ahead, respecters of life, despisers of death, the real English whereas an alienated Celtic satirist, through his vivid fancy and his disesteem, saw the country incarnate in Bull, at most a roguish screw-kneed clown to be whipped out of him. Celt and Saxon are much inmixed with us, but the prevalence of Saxon blood is evinced by the public disregard of any Celtic conception of the honourable and the loveable; so that the Celt anxious to admire is rebutted, and the hatred of a Celt, quick as he is to catch at images, has a figure of hugeous animalism supplied to his malign contempt. Rockney's historic England, and the living heroic England to slip from that dull hide in a time of trial, whether of war or social suffering, he cannot see, nor a people hardening to Spartan lineaments in the fire, iron men to meet disaster, worshippers of a discerned God of Laws, and just men too, thinking to do justice; he has Bull on the eye, the alternately braggart and poltroon, sweating in labour that he may gorge the fruits, graceless to a scoffer. And this is the creature to whose tail he is tied! Hereditary hatred is approved by critical disgust. Some spirited brilliancy, some persistent generosity (other than the guzzle's flash of it), might soften him; something sweeter than the slow animal well-meaningness his placable brethren point his attention to. It is not seen, and though he can understand the perils of a severance, he prefers to rub the rawness of his wound and be ready to pitch his cap in the air for it, out of sheer bloodloathing of a connection that offers him nothing to admire, nothing to hug to his heart. Both below and above the blind mass of discontent in his island, the repressed sentiment of admiration-or passion of fealty and thirst to give himself to a visible brighter—is an element of the division: meditative young Patrick O'Donnell early in his reflections had noted that:—and it is partly a result of our daily habit of tossing the straw to the monetary world and doting on ourselves in the mirror, until our habitual doings are viewed in a bemused complacency by us, and the scum-surface of the country is flashed about as its vital being. A man of forethought using the Press to spur Parliament to fitly represent the people, and writing on his daily topics with strenuous original vigour, even though, like Rockney, he sets the teeth of the Celt gnashing at him, goes a step nearer to the bourne of pacification than Press and Parliament reflecting the popular opinion that law must be passed to temper Ireland's eruptiveness; for that man can be admired, and the Celt, in combating him, will like an able and gallant enemy better than a grudgingly just, lumbersome, dull, politic friend. The material points in a division are always the stronger, but the sentimental are here very strong. Pass the laws; they may put an extinguisher on the Irish Vesuvian; yet to be loved you must be a little perceptibly admirable. You may be so self-satisfied as to dispense with an ideal: your yoke-fellow is not; it is his particular form of strength to require one for his proper blooming, and he does bloom beautifully in the rays he courts.

Ah then, seek to be loved, and banish Bull. Believe in a future and banish that gross obscuration of you. Decline to let that old-yeoman-turned alderman stand any longer for the national man. Speaking to the brain of the country, one is sure of the power of a resolute sign from it to dismiss the brainless. Banish him your revels and your debatings, prohibit him your Christmas, lend no ear either to his panics or his testiness, especially none to his rages; do not report him at all, and he will soon subside into his domestic, varied by pothouse, privacy. The brain should lead, if there be a brain. Once free of him, you will know that for half a century you have appeared bottom upward to mankind. And you have wondered at the absence of love for you under so astounding a presentation. Even in a Bull, beneficent as he can dream of being, when his notions are in a similar state of inversion, should be sheepish in hope for love.

He too, whom you call the Welshman, and deride for his delight in songful gatherings, harps to wild Wales, his Cambrian highlands, and not to England. You have not yet, though he is orderly and serviceable, allured his imagination to the idea of England. Despite the passion for his mountains and the boon of your raising of the interdict (within a hundred years) upon his pastors to harangue him in his native tongue, he gladly ships himself across the waters traversed by his Prince Madoc of tradition, and becomes contentedly a transatlantic citizen, a member of strange sects—he so inveterate in faithfulness to the hoar and the legendary!—Anything rather than Anglican. The Cymry bear you no hatred; their affection likewise is undefined. But there is reason to think that America has caught the imagination of the Cambrian Celt: names of Welshmen are numerous in the small army of the States of the Union; and where men take soldier-service they are usually fixed, they and their children. Here is one, not very deeply injured within a century, of ardent temperament, given to be songful and loving; he leaves you and forgets you. Be certain that the material grounds of division are not all. To pronounce it his childishness provokes the retort upon your presented shape. He cannot admire it. Gaelic Scots wind the same note of repulsion.

And your poets are in a like predicament. Your poets are the most persuasive of springs to a lively general patriotism. They are in the Celtic dilemma of standing at variance with Bull; they return him his hearty antipathy, are unable to be epical or lyrical of him, are condemned to expend their genius upon the abstract, the quaint, the picturesque. Nature they read spiritually or sensually, always shrinkingly apart from him. They swell to a resemblance of their patron if they stoop to woo his purse. He has, on hearing how that poets bring praise to nations, as in fact he can now understand his Shakespeare to have done, been seen to thump the midriff and rally them for their shyness of it, telling them he doubts them true poets while they abstain from singing him to the world-him, and the things refreshing the centre of him. Ineffectual is that encouragement. Were he in the fire, melting to the iron man, the backbone of him, it would be different. At his pleasures he is anti-hymnic, repellent to song. He has perceived the virtues of Peace, without the brother eye for the need of virtuousness to make good use of them and inspire the poet. His own enrolled unrhythmical bardic troops (humorous mercenaries when Celts) do his trumpeting best, and offend not the Pierides.

This interlude, or rather inter-drone, repulsive to write, can hardly be excluded from a theme dramatising Celtic views, and treating of a blood, to which the idea of country must shine resplendently if we would have it running at full tide through the arteries. Preserve your worship, if the object fills your optics. Better worship that than nothing, as it is better for flames to be blown out than not to ascend, otherwise it will wreak circular mischief instead of illumining. You are requested simply to recollect that there is another beside you who sees the object obliquely, and then you will not be surprised by his irreverence. What if, in the end, you were conducted to a like point of view? Self-worship, it has been said, is preferable to no trimming of the faculty, but worship does not necessarily cease with the extinction of this of the voraciously carnal. An ideal of country, of Great Britain, is conceivable that will be to the taste of Celt and

Saxon in common, to wave as a standard over their fraternal marching. Let Bull boo his drumliest at such talk: it is, I protest, the thing we want and can have. He is the obstruction, not the country; and against him, not against the country, the shots are aimed which seem so malignant. Him the gay manipulators propitiate who look at him through Literature and the Press, and across the pulpit-cushions, like airy Macheath at Society, as carrion to batten on. May plumpness be their portion, and they never hanged for it! But the flattering, tickling, pleasantly pinching of Bull is one of those offices which the simple starveling piper regards with afresh access of appetite for the well-picked bone of his virtue. That ghastly apparition of the fleshly present is revealed to him as a dead whale, having the harpoon of the inevitable slayer of the merely fleshly in his oils. To humour him, and be his piper for his gifts, is to descend to a carnival deep underneath. While he reigns, thinks this poor starveling, Rome burns, or the explosive powders are being secretly laid. He and his thousand Macheaths are dancing the country the giddy pace, and there will, the wretch dreads, be many a crater of scoria in the island, before he stretches his inanimate length, his parasites upon him. The theme is chosen and must be treated as a piper involved in his virtue conceives it: that is, realistically; not with Bull's notion of the realism of the butcher's shop and the pendent legs of mutton and blocks of beef painted raw and glaring in their streaks, but with the realism of the active brain and heart conjoined. The reasons for the division of Celt and Saxon, what they think and say of one another, often without knowing that they are divided, and the wherefore of our abusing of ourselves, brave England, our England of the ancient fortitude and the future incarnation, can afford to hear. Why not in a tale? It is he, your all for animal pleasure in the holiday he devours and cannot enjoy, whose example teaches you to shun the plaguey tale that carries fright: and so you find him sour at business and sick of his relaxings, hating both because he harnesses himself in turn bestially to each, growling at the smallest admixture of them, when, if he would but chirp a little over his work, and allow his pleasures to inspire a dose of thoughtfulness, he would be happier, and—who knows?-become a brighter fellow, one to be rescued from the pole-axe.

Now the rain is over, your carriage is at the door, the country smiles and the wet highway waves a beckoning hand. We have worn through a cloud with cloudy discourses, but we are in a land of shifting weathers, 'coelum crebris imbribus ac nebulis foedum,' not every chapter can be sunshine.

CHAPTER XVII. CROSSING THE RUBICON

Rough weather on the Irish sea discharged a pallid file of passengers from the boat at Holyhead just as the morning sun struck wave and mountain with one of the sudden sparkling changes which our South-welters have in their folds to tell us after a tumultuous night that we have only been worried by Puck. The scene of frayed waters all rosy-golden, and golden-banded heathery height, with the tinted sand, breaking to flights of blue, was resplendent for those of our recent sea-farers who could lift an eye to enjoy it. Freshness, illumination, then salt air, vivid distances, were a bath for every sense of life. You could believe the breast of the mountain to be heaving, the billows to be kissing fingers to him, the rollers shattered up the cliff to have run to extinction to scale him. He seemed in his clear-edged mass King of this brave new boundless world built in a minute out of the wreck of the old.

An hour back the vessel was labouring through rueful chasms under darkness, and then did the tricksy Southwest administer grisly slaps to right and left, whizzing spray across the starboard beam, and drenching the locks of a young lady who sat cloaked and hooded in frieze to teach her wilfulness a lesson, because she would keep her place on deck from beginning to end of the voyage. Her faith in the capacity of Irish frieze to turn a deluge of the deeps driven by an Atlantic gale was shaken by the time she sighted harbour, especially when she shed showers by flapping a batlike wing of the cloak, and had a slight shudder to find herself trickling within.

'Dear! and I'm wet to the skin,' she confided the fact to herself vocally.

'You would not be advised,' a gentleman beside her said after a delicate pause to let her impulsive naturalism of utterance fly by unwounded.

'And aren't you the same and worse? And not liking it either, I fear, Sir!' she replied, for despite a manful smile his complexion was tell-tale. 'But there 's no harm in salt. But you should have gone down to the cabin with Father Boyle and you would have been sure of not catching cold. But, Oh! the beautiful... look at it! And it's my first view of England. Well, then, I'll say it's a beautiful country.'

Her companion looked up at the lighted sky, and down at the pools in tarpaulin at his feet. He repressed a disposition to shudder, and with the anticipated ecstasy of soon jumping out of wet clothes into dry, he said: 'I should like to be on the top of that hill now.'

The young lady's eyes flew to the top.

'They say he looks on Ireland; I love him; and his name is Caer Gybi; and it was one of our Saints gave him the name, I 've read in books. I'll be there before noon.'

'You want to have a last gaze over to Erin?'

'No, it's to walk and feel the breeze. But I do, though.'

'Won't you require a little rest?'

'Sure and I've had it sitting here all night!' said she.

He laughed: the reason for the variation of exercise was conclusive.

Father Boyle came climbing up the ladder, uncertain of his legs; he rolled and snatched and tottered on his way to them, and accepted the gentleman's help of an arm, saying: 'Thank ye, thank ye, and good morning, Mr. Colesworth. And my poor child! what sort of a night has it been above, Kathleen?'

He said it rather twinkling, and she retorted:

'What sort of a night has it been below, Father Boyle?' Her twinkle was livelier than his, compassionate in archness.

'Purgatory past is good for contemplation, my dear. 'Tis past, and there's the comfort! You did well to be out of that herring-barrel, Mr. Colesworth. I hadn't the courage, or I would have burst from it to take a ducking with felicity. I haven't thrown up my soul; that's the most I can say. I thought myself nigh on it once or twice. And an amazing kind steward it was, or I'd have counted the man for some one else. Surely 'tis a glorious morning?'

Mr. Colesworth responded heartily in praise of the morning. He was beginning to fancy that he felt the warmth of spring sunshine on his back. He flung up his head and sniffed the air, and was very like a horse fretful for the canter; so like as to give Miss Kathleen an idea of the comparison. She could have rallied him; her laughing eyes showed the readiness, but she forbore, she drank the scene. Her face, with the threaded locks about forehead and cheeks, and the dark, the blue, the rosy red of her lips, her eyes, her hair, was just such a south-western sky as April drove above her, the same in colour and quickness; and much of her spirit was the same, enough to stand for a resemblance. But who describes the spirit? No one at the gates of the field of youth. When Time goes reaping he will gather us a sheaf, out of which the picture springs.

'There's our last lurch, glory to the breakwater!' exclaimed Father Boyle, as the boat pitched finally outside the harbour fence, where a soft calm swell received them with the greeting of civilised sea-nymphs. 'The captain'll have a quieter passage across. You may spy him on the pier. We'll be meeting him on the landing.'

'If he's not in bed, from watching the stars all night,' said Miss Kathleen.

'He must have had a fifty-lynx power of sight for that, my dear.'

'They did appear, though, and wonderfully bright,' she said. 'I saw them come out and go in. It's not all cloud when the high wind blows.'

'You talk like a song, Kathleen.'

'Couldn't I rattle a throat if I were at home, Father!'

'Ah! we're in the enemy's country now.'

Miss Kathleen said she would go below to get the handbags from the stewardess.

Mr. Colesworth's brows had a little darkened over the Rev. Gentleman's last remark. He took two or three impatient steps up and down with his head bent. 'Pardon me; I hoped we had come to a better understanding,' he said. 'Is it quite fair to the country and to Miss O'Donnell to impress on her before she knows us that England is the enemy?'

'Habit, Mr. Colesworth, habit! we've got accustomed to the perspective and speak accordingly. There's a breach visible.'

'I thought you agreed with me that good efforts are being made on our side to mend the breach.'

'Sir, you have a noble minority at work, no doubt; and I take you for one of the noblest, as not objecting to stand next to alone.'

'I really thought, judging from our conversation at Mrs. O'Donnell's that evening, that you were going to hold out a hand and lead your flock to the right sort of fellowship with us.'

'To submission to the laws, Mr. Colesworth; 'tis my duty to do it as pastor and citizen.'

'No, to more than that, sir. You spoke with friendly warmth.'

'The atmosphere was genial, if you remember the whisky and the fumes of our tobacco at one o'clock!'

'I shall recollect the evening with the utmost pleasure. You were kind enough to instruct me in a good many things I shall be sure to profit by. I wish I could have spent more time in Ireland. As it is, I like Irishmen so well that if the whole land were in revolt I should never call it the enemy's country.'

'Excellently spoken, Mr. Colesworth,' said the priest. 'We 'll hope your writings may do service to mend the breach. For there is one, as you know, and more 's the pity; there's one, and it's wide and deep. As my friend Captain Con O'Donnell says, it's plain to the naked eye as a pair of particularly fat laundry drawers hung out to dry and ballooned in extension—if mayhap you've ever seen the sight of them in that state:—just held together by a narrow neck of thread or button, and stretching away like a corpulent frog in the act of swimming on the wind. His comparison touches the sentiment of disunion, sir.'

Mr. Colesworth had not ever seen such a pair of laundry drawers inflated to symbolise the breach between Ireland and England; nor probably, if he had, would the sentiment of national disunion have struck his mind: it was difficult to him in the description. He considered his Rev. friend to be something of a slippery fish, while Father Boyle's opinion of him likewise referred him to an elemental substance, of slow movement-earth, in short: for he continued to look argumentative after all had been said.

Or perhaps he threw a coveting eye on sweet Miss Kathleen and had his own idea of mending a stitch of the breach in a quite domestic way. If so, the Holy Father would have a word to say, let alone Kathleen. The maids of his Church do not espouse her foes. For the men it is another matter: that is as the case may be. Temporarily we are in cordial intercourse, Mr. Colesworth.

Miss Kathleen returned to deck carrying her bags. The gentleman had to descend, and subsequently an amiable dissension arose on the part of the young lady and Mr. Colesworth. She, however, yielded one of her bags, and he, though doubly laden, was happy. All very transparent to pastoral observation, but why should they not be left to their chirruping youthfulness? The captain was not in view, and Father Boyle wanted to go to bed for refreshment, and Kathleen was an airy gossamer, with a boy running after it, not by any means likely to catch it, or to keep it if he did. Proceed and trip along, you young ones!

At the hotel they heard that Captain Con O'Donnell was a snug sleeper upstairs. This, the captain himself very soon informed them, had not been the kernel of the truth. He had fancied they would not cross the Channel on so rattlesome a night, or Kathleen would have had an Irish kiss to greet her landing in England. But the cousinly salute was little delayed, news of the family in Ireland and England was exchanged, and then Mr. Colesworth and the captain bowed to an introduction; and the captain, at mention of his name, immediately cried out that Mr.

Colesworth might perchance be a relative of the highly intelligent admirable lady who had undertaken the secretaryship, and by her vast ability got the entire management, of Miss Mattock's benevolent institution, and was conducting it with such success that it was fast becoming a grief to the generous heart of the foundress of the same to find it not only self-paying, but on the road to a fortune, inasmuch as it was already an article in the decrees of fashion among the nobility and gentry of both sexes in the metropolis to have their linen and laces washed at the Mattock laundry.

Mr. Colesworth said he was the brother of the lady in question, he had also the pleasure of an acquaintance with Miss Mattock. He was vehemently congratulated on the relationship, which bore witness, the captain armed, to a certain hereditary share of brains greatly to be envied: brother of Miss Colesworth, a title of distinction in itself! He was congratulated not less cordially for his being so fortunate as to know Miss Mattock, one of a million.

Captain Con retained the hand of Father Boyle and squeezed it during his eulogies, at the same time dispensing nods and winks and sunny sparkles upon Kathleen. Mr. Colesworth went upstairs to his room not unflattered. The flattery enveloped him in the pleasant sense of a somehow now established companionship for the day with a pleasant person from whom he did not wish to separate.

'You made the gentleman's acquaintance, my dear...?' said Con.

Kathleen answered: 'He made friends with our Patrick on the Continent, I think it was in Germany, and came to us to study the old country, bearing a letter from Patrick. He means to be one of their writers on the newspapers. He studies everything; he has written books. He called on us coming and called on us going and we came over together,' said Miss Kathleen. 'But tell me: our Philip?'

'Books!' Con exclaimed. 'It's hard to discover a man in these days who hasn't written books. Oh! Philip! Ease your heart about Philip. They're nursing him, round. He was invalided at the right moment for him, no fear. I gave him his chance of the last vacant seat up to the last hour, and now the die is cast and this time I'm off to it. Poor Philip—yes, yes! we're sorry to see him flat all his length, we love him; he's a gallant soldier; alive to his duty; and that bludgeon sun of India knocked him down, and that fall from his horse finished the business, and there he lies. But he'll get up, and he might have accepted the seat and spared me my probation: he's not married, I am, I have a wife, and Master Philip divides me against my domestic self, he does. But let that be: I serve duty too. Not a word to our friend up yonder. It's a secret with a time-fuse warranted to explode safe enough when the minutes are up, and make a powerful row when it does. It is all right over there, Father Boyle, I suppose?'

'A walk over! a pure ceremonial,' said the priest, and he yawned frightfully.

'You're for a nap to recompose you, my dear friend,' remarked the captain.

'But you haven't confided anything of it to Mrs. Adister?'

'Not a syllable; no. That's to come. There's my contest! I had urgent business in Ireland, and she's a good woman, always willing to let me go. I count on her kindness, there's no mightier compliment to one's wife. She'll know it when it's history. She's fond of history. Ay, she hates fiction, and so I'm proud to tell her I offer her none. She likes a trifling surprise too, and there she has it. Oh! we can whip up the business to a nice little bowl of froth-flummery. But it's when the Parliamentary voting is on comes the connubial pull. She's a good woman, a dear good soul, but she's a savage patriot; and Philip might have saved his kinsman if he had liked. He had only to say the word: I could have done all the business for him, and no contest to follow by my fireside. He's on his couch—Mars convalescent: a more dreadful attraction to the ladies than in his crimson plumes! If the fellow doesn't let slip his opportunity! with his points of honour and being an Irish Bayard. Why Bayard in the nineteenth century's a Bedlamite, Irish or no. So I tell him. There he is; you'll see him, Kathleen: and one of them as big an heiress as any in England. Philip's no fool, you'll find.'

'Then he's coming all right, is he?' said Kathleen.

'He 's a soldier, and a good one, but he 's nothing more, and as for patriotic inflammation, doesn't know the sensation.'

'Oh! but he's coming round, and you'll go and stroke down mother with that,' Kathleen cried. 'Her heart's been heavy, with Patrick wandering and Philip on his back. I'll soon be dressed for breakfast.'

Away she went.

'She's got an appetite, and looks like a strapped bit of steel after the night's tumbling,' said the captain, seeing her trip aloft. 'I'm young as that too, or not far off it. Stay, I'll order breakfast for four in a quiet corner where we can converse—which, by the way, won't be possible in the presence of that gaping oyster of a fellow, who looks as if he were waiting the return of the tide.'

Father Boyle interposed his hand.

'Not for...' he tried to add 'four.' The attempt at a formation of the word produced a cavernous yawn a volume of the distressful deep to the beholder.

'Of course,' Captain Con assented. He proposed bed and a sedative therein, declaring that his experience overnight could pronounce it good, and that it should be hot. So he led his tired old friend to the bedroom, asked dozens of questions, flurried a withdrawal of them, suggested the answers, talked of his Rubicon, praised his wife, delivered a moan on her behalf, and after assisting to half disrobe the scarce animate figure, which lent itself like an artist's lay-model to the operation, departed on his mission of the sedative.

At the breakfast for three he was able to tell Kathleen that the worthy Father was warm, and on his way to complete restoration.

'Full fathom five the Father lies, in the ocean of sleep, by this time,' said Con. 'And 'tis a curious fact that every man in that condition seems enviable to men on their legs. And similarly with death; we'd rather not, because of a qualm, but the picture of the finish of the leap across is a taking one. These chops are done as if Nature had mellowed their juiciness.'

'They are so nice,' Kathleen said.

'You deserve them, if ever girl in this world!'

'I sat on deck all night, and Mr. Colesworth would keep me company.'

'He could hardly do less, having the chance. But that notwithstanding, I'm under an obligation to your cavalier. And how did you find Ireland, sir? You've made acquaintance with my cousin, young Mr. Patrick O'Donnell, I rejoice to hear.'

'Yes, through his hearing or seeing my name and suspecting I had a sister,' said Mr. Colesworth, who was no longer in the resemblance of a gaping oyster on the borders of the ebb. 'The country is not disturbed.'

'So the doctor thinks his patient is doing favourably! And you cottoned to Patrick? And I don't wonder. Where was it?'

'We met in Trieste. He was about to start by one of the Austrian boats for the East.'

'Not disturbed! no! with a rotten potato inside it paralysing digestion!' exclaimed Con. 'Now Patrick had been having a peep at Vienna, hadn't he?'

'He had; he was fresh from Vienna when I met him. As to Ireland, the harvest was only middling good last year.'

'And that's the bit of luck we depend on. A cloud too much, and it's drowned! Had he seen, do you know, anybody in Vienna?—you were not long together at Trieste?'

Mr. Colesworth had sufficient quickness to perceive that the two questions could be answered as one, and saying: 'He was disappointed,' revealed that he and Patrick had been long enough together to come to terms of intimacy.

'To be sure, he gave you a letter of introduction to his family!' said Con. 'And permit me to add, that Patrick's choice of a friend is mine on trust. The lady he was for seeing, Mr. Colesworth, was just then embarking on an adventure of a romantic character, particularly well suited to her nature, and the end of it was a trifle sanguinary, and she suffered a disappointment also, though not perhaps on that account.'

'I heard of it in England last year,' said Mr. Colesworth. 'Did she come through it safely?'

'Without any personal disfigurement: and is in England now, under her father's roof, meditating fresh adventures.'

Kathleen cried: 'Ye 're talking of the lady who was Miss Adister—I can guess—Ah!' She humped her shoulders and sent a shudder up her neck.

'But she's a grand creature, Mr. Colesworth, and you ought to know her,' said Con. 'That is, if you'd like to have an idea of a young Catherine or a Semiramisminus an army and a country. There's nothing she's not capable of aiming at. And there's pretty well nothing and nobody she wouldn't make use of. She has great notions of the power of the British Press and the British purse—each in turn as a key to the other. Now for an egg, Kathleen.'

'I think I'll eat an egg,' Kathleen replied.

'Bless the honey heart of the girl! Life's in you, my dear, and calls for fuel. I'm glad to see that Mr. Colesworth too can take a sight at the Sea-God after a night of him. It augurs magnificently for a future career. And let me tell you that the Pen demands it of us. The first of the requisites is a stout stomach—before a furnished head! I'd not pass a man to be anything of a writer who couldn't step ashore from a tempest and consume his Titan breakfast.'

'We are qualifying for the literary craft, Miss O'Donnell,' said Mr. Colesworth.

'It's for a walk in the wind up Caer Gybi, and along the coast I mean to go,' said Kathleen.

'This morning?' the captain asked her.

She saw his dilemma in his doubtful look.

'When I've done. While you're discussing matters with Father Boyle. I—know you're burning to. Sure it's yourself knows as well as anybody, Captain Con, that I can walk a day long and take care of my steps. I've walked the better half of Donegal alone, and this morning I'll have a protector.'

Captain Con eyed the protector, approved of him, disapproved of himself, thought of Kathleen as a daughter of Erin—a privileged and inviolate order of woman in the minds of his countrymen—and wriggling internally over a remainder scruple said: 'Mr. Colesworth mayhap has to write a bit in the morning.'

'I'm unattached at present,' the latter said. 'I am neither a correspondent nor a reporter, and if I were, the event would be wanting.'

'That remark, sir, shows you to be eminently a stranger to the official duties,' observed the captain. 'Journalism is a maw, and the journalist has to cram it, and like anything else which perpetually distends for matter, it must be filled, for you can't leave it gaping, so when nature and circumstance won't combine to produce the stuff, we have recourse to the creative arts. 'Tis the necessity of the profession.'

'The profession will not impose that necessity upon me,' remarked the young practitioner.

'Outside the wheels of the machine, sir, we indulge our hallucination of immunity. I've been one in the whirr of them, relating what I hadn't quite heard, and capitulating what I didn't think at all, in spite of the cry of my conscience—a poor infant below the waters, casting up ejaculatory bubbles of protestation. And if it is my reproach that I left it to the perils of drowning, it's my pride that I continued to transmit air enough to carry on the struggle. Not every journalist can say as much. The Press is the voice of the mass, and our private opinion is detected as a discord by the mighty beast, and won't be endured by him.'

'It's better not to think of him quite as a beast,' said Mr. Colesworth.

'Infinitely better: and I like your "guile," sir: But wait and tell me what you think of him after tossing him his meat for a certain number of years. There's Rockney. Do you know Rockney? He's the biggest single gun they've got, and he's mad for this country, but ask him about the public, you'll hear the menagerie-keeper's opinion of the brute that mauled his loins.'

'Rockney,' said Mr. Colesworth, 'has the tone of a man disappointed of the dictatorship.'

'Then you do know Rockney!' shouted Captain Con. 'That's the man in a neat bit of drawing. He's a grand piece of ordnance. But wait for him too, and tell me by and by. If it isn't a woman, you'll find, that primes him, ay, and points him, and what's more, discharges him, I'm not Irish born. Poor fellow! I pity him. He had a sweet Irish lady for his wife, and lost her last year, and has been raging astray politically ever since. I suppose it's hardly the poor creature's fault. None the less, you know, we have to fight him. And now he's nibbling at a bait—it's fun: the lady I mentioned, with a turn for adventure and enterprise: it's rare fun: he's nibbling, he'll be hooked. You must make her acquaintance, Mr. Colesworth, and hold your own against her, if you can. She's a niece of my wife's and I'll introduce you. I shall find her in London, or at our lodgings at a Surrey farm we've taken to nurse my cousin Captain Philip O'Donnell invalided from Indian awful climate!—on my return, when I hope to renew the acquaintance. She has beauty, she has brains. Resist her, and you 'll make a decent stand against Lucifer. And supposing she rolls you up and pitches you over, her noticing you is a pretty compliment to your pen. That 'll be consoling.'

Mr. Colesworth fancied, he said, that he was proof against feminine blandishments in the direction of his writings.

He spoke as one indicating a thread to suggest a cable. The captain applauded the fancy as a pleasing delusion of the young sprigs of Journalism.

Upon this, Mr. Colesworth, with all respect for French intelligence, denied the conclusiveness of French generalisations, which ascribed to women universal occult dominion, and traced all great affairs to small intrigues.

The captain's eyes twinkled on him, thinking how readily he would back smart Miss Kathleen to do the trick, if need were.

He said to her before she started: 'Don't forget he may be a clever fellow with that pen of his, and useful to our party.'

'I'll not forget,' said she.

For the good of his party, then, Captain Con permitted her to take the walk up Caer Gybi alone with Mr. Colesworth: a memorable walk in the recollections of the scribe, because of the wonderful likeness of the young lady to the breezy weather and the sparkles over the deep, the cloud that frowned, the cloud that glowed, the green of the earth greening out from under wings of shadow, the mountain ranges holding hands about an immensity of space. It was one of our giant days to his emotions, and particularly memorable to him through the circumstance that it insisted on a record in verse, and he was unused to the fetters of metre: and although the verse was never seen by man, his attempt at it confused his ideas of his expressive powers. Oddly too, while scourging the lines with criticism, he had a fondness for them: they stamped a radiant day in his mind, beyond the resources of rhetoric to have done it equally.

This was the day of Captain Con's crossing the Rubicon between the secret of his happiness and a Parliamentary career.

CHAPTER XVIII. CAPTAIN CON'S LETTER

Women may be able to tell you why the nursing of a military invalid awakens tenderer anxieties in their bosoms than those called forth by the drab civilian. If we are under sentence of death we are all of us pathetic of course; but stretched upon the debateable couch of sickness we are not so touching as the coloured coat: it has the distinction belonging to colour. It smites a deeper nerve, or more than one; and this, too, where there is no imaginary subjection to the charms of military glory, in minds to which the game of war is lurid as the plumes of the arch-slayer.

Jane Mattock assisting Mrs. Adister O'Donnell to restore Captain Philip was very singularly affected, like a person shut off on a sudden from her former theories and feelings. Theoretically she despised the soldier's work as much as she shrank abhorrently from bloodshed. She regarded him and his trappings as an ensign of our old barbarism, and could peruse platitudes upon that theme with enthusiasm. The soldier personally, she was accustomed to consider an inferior intelligence: a sort of schoolboy when young, and schoolmaster when mature a visibly limited creature, not a member of our broader world. Without dismissing any of these views she found them put aside for the reception of others of an opposite character; and in her soul she would have ascribed it to her cares of nursing that she had become thoughtful, doubtful, hopeful, even prayerful, surcharged with zeal, to help to save a good sword for the country. If in a world still barbarous we must have soldiers, here was one whom it would be grievous to lose. He had fallen for the country; and there was a moving story of how he had fallen. She inclined to think more highly of him for having courted exposure on a miserable frontier war where but a poor sheaf of glory could be gathered. And he seemed to estimate his professional duties apart from an aim at the laurels. A conception of the possibility of a man's being both a soldier and morally a hero edged its way into her understanding. It stood edgeways within, desirous of avoiding a challenge to show every feature.

The cares of nursing were Jane's almost undividedly, except for the aid she had from her friend Grace Barrow and from Miss Colesworth. Mrs. Adister O'Donnell was a nurse in name only. 'She'll be seen by Philip like as if she were a nightmare apparition of his undertaker's wraith,' Captain Con said to Jane, when recommending his cousin to her charitable nature, after he had taken lodgings at a farmhouse near Mrs. Lackstraw's model farm Woodside on the hills. 'Barring the dress,' as he added, some such impression of her frigid mournfulness might have struck a recumbent invalid. Jane acknowledged it, and at first induced her aunt to join her in the daily walk of half a mile to sit with him. Mrs. Lackstraw was a very busy lady at her farm; she was often summoned to London by her intuition of John's wish to have her presiding at table for the entertainment of his numerous guests; she confessed that she supervised the art of nursing better than she practised it, and supervision can be done at a distance if the subordinate is properly attentive to the rules we lay down, as Jane appeared to be. So Jane was left to him. She loved the country; Springtide in the country set her singing; her walk to her patient at Lappett's farm and homeward was an aethereal rapture for a heart rocking easy in fulness. There was nothing to trouble it, no hint of wild winds and heavy seas, not even the familiar insinuation from the vigilant monitress, her aunt, to bid her be on her guard, beware of what it is that great heiresses are courted for, steel her heart against serpent speeches, see well to have the woman's precious word No at the sentinel's post, and alert there. Mrs. Lackstraw, the most vigilant and plain-spoken of her sex, had forborne to utter the usual warnings which were to preserve Miss Mattock for her future Earl or Duke and the reason why she forbore was a double one; a soldier and Papist could never be thought perilous to a young woman scorning the sons of Mars and slaves of sacerdotalism. The picture of Jane bestowing her hand on a Roman Catholic in military uniform, refused to be raised before the mind. Charitableness, humaneness, the fact that she was an admirable nurse and liked to exercise her natural gift, perfectly accounted for Jane's trips to Lappett's farm, and the jellies and fresh dairy dainties and neat little dishes she was constantly despatching to the place. A suggestion of possible danger might prove more dangerous than silence, by rendering it attractive. Besides, Jane talked of poor Captain Philip as Patrick O'Donnell's brother, whom she was bound to serve in return for Patrick's many services to her; and of how unlike Patrick he was. Mrs. Lackstraw had been apprehensive about her fancy for Patrick. Therefore if Captain Philip was unlike him, and strictly a Catholic, according to report, the suspicion of danger dispersed, and she was allowed to enjoy the pleasures of the metropolis as frequently as she chose. The nursing of a man of Letters, or of the neighbour to him, a beggar in rags, would not have been so tolerated. Thus we perceive that wits actively awake inside the ring-fence of prepossessions they have erected may lull themselves with their wakefulness. Who would have thought!—is the cry when the strongest bulwark of the fence is broken through.

Jane least of any would have thought what was coming to pass. The pale square-browed young officer, so little Irish and winning in his brevity of speech, did and said nothing to alarm her or strike the smallest light. Grace Barrow noticed certain little changes of mood in Jane she could scarcely have had a distinct suspicion at the time. After a recent observation of him, on an evening stroll from Lappett's to Woodside, she pronounced him interesting, but hard. 'He has an interesting head... I should not like to offend him.' They agreed as to his unlikeness to fluid Patrick; both eulogistic of the absent brother; and Jane, who could be playful in privacy with friends, clapped a brogue on her tongue to discourse of Patrick and apostrophise him: 'Oh! Pat, Pat, my dear cousin Pat! why are you so long away from your desponding Jane? I'll take to poetry and write songs, if you don't come home soon. You've put seas between us, and are behaving to me as an enemy. I know you'll bring home a foreign Princess to break the heart of your faithful. But I'll always praise you for a dear boy, Pat, and wish you happy, and beg the good gentleman your brother to give me a diploma as nurse to your first-born. There now!'

She finished smiling brightly, and Grace was a trifle astonished, for her friend's humour was not as a rule dramatic.

'You really have caught a twang of it from your friend Captain Con; only you don't rattle the eighteenth letter of the alphabet in the middle of words.'

'I've tried, and can't persuade my tongue to do it "first off," as boys say, and my invalid has no brogue whatever to keep me in practice,' Jane replied. 'One wonders what he thinks of as he lies there by the window. He doesn't confide it to his hospital nurse.'

'Yes, he would treat her courteously, just in that military style,' said Grace, realising the hospital attendance.

'It's the style I like best:—no perpetual personal thankings and allusions to the trouble he gives!' Jane exclaimed. 'He shows perfect good sense, and I like that in all things, as you know. A red-haired young woman chooses to wait on him and bring him flowers—he's brother to Patrick in his love of wild flowers, at all events!—and he takes it naturally and simply. These officers bear illness well. I suppose it's the drill.'

'Still I think it a horrid profession, dear.'

Grace felt obliged to insist on that: and her 'I think,' though it was not stressed, tickled Jane's dormant ear to some drowsy wakefulness.

'I think too much honour is paid to it, certainly. But soldiers, of all men, one would expect to be overwhelmed by a feeling of weakness. He has never complained; not once. I doubt if he would have complained if Mrs. Adister had been waiting on him all the while, or not a soul. I can imagine him lying on the battle-field night after night quietly, resolving not to groan.'

'Too great a power of self-repression sometimes argues the want of any emotional nature,' said Grace.

Jane shook her head. She knew a story of him contradicting that.

The story had not recurred to her since she had undertaken her service. It coloured the remainder of an evening walk home through the beechwoods and over the common with Grace, and her walk across the same tracks early in the morning, after Grace had gone to London. Miss Colesworth was coming to her next week, with her brother if he had arrived in England. Jane remembered having once been curious about this adventurous man of Letters who lived by the work of his pen. She remembered comparing him to one who was compelled to swim perpetually without a ship to give him rest or land in view. He had made a little money by a book, and was expending it on travels—rather imprudently, she fancied Emma Colesworth to be thinking. He talked well, but for the present she was happier in her prospect of nearly a week of loneliness. The day was one of sunshine, windless, odorous: one of the rare placid days of April when the pettish month assumes a matronly air of summer and wears it till the end of the day. The beech twigs were strongly embrowned, the larches shot up green spires by the borders of woods and on mounds within, deep ditchbanks unrolled profuse tangles of new blades, and sharp eyes might light on a late white violet overlooked by the children; primroses ran along the banks. Jane had a maxim that flowers should be spared to live their life, especially flowers of the wilds; she had reared herself on our poets; hence Mrs. Lackstraw's dread of the arrival of one of the minstrel order: and the girl, who could deliberately cut a bouquet from the garden, if requested, would refuse to pluck a wildflower. But now they cried out to her to be plucked in hosts, they claimed the sacrifice, and it seemed to her no violation of her sentiment to gather handfuls making a bunch that would have done honour to the procession of the children's May-day—a day she excused for the slaughter because her idol and prophet among the poets, wild nature's interpreter, was that day on the side of the children. How like a bath of freshness would the thick faintly-fragrant mass shine to her patient! Only to look at it was medicine! She believed, in her lively healthfulness, that the look would give him a spring to health, and she hurried forward to have them in water-the next sacred obligation to the leaving of them untouched.

She had reared herself on our poets. If much brooding on them will sometimes create a sentimentalism of the sentiment they inspire, that also, after our manner of developing, leads to finer civilisation; and as her very delicate feelings were not always tyrants over her clear and accurate judgement, they rather tended to stamp her character than lead her into foolishness. Blunt of speech, quick in sensibility, imaginative, yet idealistic, she had the complex character of diverse brain and nerve, and was often a problem to the chief person interested in it. She thought so decisively, felt so shrinkingly; spoke so flatly, brooded so softly! Such natures, in the painful effort to reconcile apparent antagonism and read themselves, forget that they are not full grown. Longer than others are they young: but meanwhile they are of an age when we are driven abroad to seek and shape our destinies.

Passing through the garden-gate of Lappett's farm she made her way to the south-western face of the house to beg a bowl of water of the farmer's wife, and had the sweet surprise of seeing her patient lying under swallows' eaves on a chair her brother had been commissioned to send from London for coming uses. He was near the farm-wife's kitchen, but to windward of the cooking-reek, pleasantly warmed, sufficiently shaded, and alone, with open letter on the rug covering his legs. He whistled to Jane's dog Wayland, a retriever, having Newfoundland relationships, of smithy redness and ruggedness; it was the whistle that startled her to turn and see him as she was in the act of handing Mrs. Lappett her primroses.

'Out? I feared it would be a week. Is it quite prudent?' Jane said, toning down her delight.

He answered with the half-smile that refers these questions to the settled fact. Air had always brought him round; now he could feel he was embarked for recovery: and he told her how the farmer and one of his men had lent a shoulder to present him to his old and surest physician—rather like a crippled ghost. M. Adister was upstairs in bed with one of her headaches. Captain Con, then, was attending her, Jane supposed: She spoke of him as the most devoted of husbands.

A slight hardening of Philip's brows, well-known to her by this time, caused her to interrogate his eyes. They were fixed on her in his manner of gazing with strong directness. She read the contrary opinion, and some hieroglyphic matter besides.

'We all respect him for his single-hearted care of her,' she said. 'I have a great liking for him. His tirades about the Saxon tyrant are not worth mentioning, they mean nothing. He would be one of the first to rush to the standard if there were danger; I know he would. He is truly chivalrous, I am sure.'

Philip's broad look at her had not swerved. The bowl of primroses placed beside him on a chair by the farmer's dame diverted it for a moment.

'You gathered them?' he said.

Jane drank his look at the flowers.

'Yes, on my way,' she replied. 'We can none of us live for ever; and fresh water every day will keep them alive a good long time. They had it from the clouds yesterday. Do they not seem a bath of country happiness!' Evidently they did their service in pleasing him.

Seeing his fingers grope on the rug, she handed him his open letters.

He selected the second, passing under his inspection, and asked her to read it.

She took the letter, wondering a little that it should be in Captain Con's handwriting.

'I am to read it through?' she said, after a run over some lines.

He nodded. She thought it a sign of his friendliness in sharing family secrets with her, and read:

'MY DEAR PHILIP,—Not a word of these contents, which will be delivered seasonably to the lady chiefly concerned, by the proper person. She hears this morning I'm off on a hasty visit to Ireland, as I have been preparing her of late to expect I must, and yours the blame, if any, though I will be the last to fling it at you. I meet Father B. and pretty Kitty before I cross. Judging by the wind this morning, the passage will furnish good schooling for a spell of the hustings. But if I am in the nature of things unable to command the waves, trust me for holding a mob in leash; and they are tolerably alike. My spirits are up. Now the die is cast. My election to the vacancy must be reckoned beforehand. I promise you a sounding report from the Kincora Herald. They will not say of me after that (and read only the speeches reported in the local paper) "what is the man but an Irish adventurer!" He is a lover of his country, Philip O'Donnell, and one of millions, we will hope. And that stigmatic title of long standing, more than anything earthly, drove him to the step- to the ruin of his domestic felicity perhaps. But we are past sighing.

'Think you, when he crossed the tide, Caius Julius Caesar sighed?

'No, nor thought of his life, nor his wife, but of the thing to be done. Laugh, my boy! I know what I am about when I set my mind on a powerful example. As the chameleon gets his colour, we get our character from the objects we contemplate...'

Jane glanced over the edge of the letter sheet rosily at Philip.

His dryness in hitting the laughable point diverted her, and her mind became suffused with a series of pictures of the chameleon captain planted in view of the Roman to become a copy of him, so that she did not peruse the terminating lines with her wakefullest attention:

'The liege lady of my heart will be the earliest to hail her hero triumphant, or cherish him beaten—which is not in the prospect. Let Ireland be true to Ireland. We will talk of the consolidation of the Union by and by. You are for that, you say, when certain things are done; and you are where I leave you, on the highway, though seeming to go at a funeral pace to certain ceremonies leading to the union of the two countries in the solidest fashion, to their mutual benefit, after a shining example. Con sleeps with a corner of the eye open, and you are not the only soldier who is a strategist, and a tactician too, aware of when it is best to be out of the way. Now adieu and pax vobiscum. Reap the rich harvest of your fall to earth. I leave you in the charge of the kindest of nurses, next to the wife of my bosom the best of women. Appreciate her, sir, or perish in my esteem. She is one whom not to love is to be guilty of an offence deserving capital punishment, and a bastinado to season the culprit for his execution. Have I not often informed her myself that a flower from her hand means more than treasures from the hands of others. Expect me absent for a week. The harangues will not be closely reported. I stand by the truth, which is my love of the land of my birth. A wife must come second to that if she would be first in her husband's consideration. Hurrah me on, Philip, now it is action, and let me fancy I hear you shouting it.'

The drop of the letter to the signature fluttered affectionately on a number of cordial adjectives, like the airy bird to his home in the corn.

CHAPTER XIX. MARS CONVALESCENT

Jane's face was clear as the sky when she handed the letter back to Philip. In doing so, it struck her that the prolonged directness of his look was peculiar: she attributed it to some effect of the fresh Spring atmosphere on a weakened frame. She was guessing at his reasons for showing her the letter, and they appeared possibly serious.

'An election to Parliament! Perhaps Mrs. Adister should have a hint of it, to soften the shock I fear it may be: but we must wait till her headache has passed,' she said.

'You read to the end?' said Philip.

'Yes, Captain Con always amuses me, and I am bound to confess I have no positive disrelish of his compliments. But this may prove a desperate step. The secret of his happiness is in extreme jeopardy. Nothing would stop him, I suppose?'

Philip signified that it was too late. He was moreover of opinion, and stated it in his briefest, that it would be advisable to leave the unfolding of the present secret to the captain.

Jane wondered why the letter had been shown. Her patient might be annoyed and needing sympathy?

'After all,' she said, 'Captain Con may turn out to be a very good sort of member of Parliament in his way.'

Philip's eyebrows lifted, and he let fall a breath, eloquent of his thoughts.

'My brother says he is a serviceable director of the Company they are associated in.'

'He finds himself among reasonable men, and he is a chameleon.'

'Parliament may steady him.'

'It is too much of a platform for Con's head.'

'Yes, there is more of poet than politician,' said she. 'That is a danger. But he calls himself our friend; I think he really has a liking for John and me.'

'For you he has a real love,' said Philip.

'Well, then, he may listen to us at times; he may be trusted not to wound us. I am unmitigatedly for the one country—no divisions. We want all our strength in these days of monstrous armies directed by banditti Councils. England is the nation of the Christian example to nations. Oh! surely it is her aim. At least she strives to be that. I think it, and I see the many faults we have.'

Her patient's eyelids were down.

She proposed to send her name up to Mrs. Adister.

On her return from the poor lady racked with headache and lying little conscious of her husband's powder-barrel under the bed, Jane found her patient being worried by his official nurse, a farm-labourer's wife, a bundle of a woman, whose lumbering assiduities he fenced with reiterated humourous negatives to every one of her propositions, until she prefaced the last two or three of the list with a 'Deary me!' addressed consolatorily to herself. She went through the same forms each day, at the usual hours of the day, and Jane, though she would have felt the apathetic doltishness of the woman less, felt how hard it must be for him to bear.

'Your sister will be with you soon,' she said. 'I am glad, and yet I hope you will not allow her to put me aside altogether?'

'You shall do as you wish,' said Philip.

'Is she like Patrick? Her name is Kathleen, I know.'

'She is a raw Irish girl, of good Irish training, but Irish.'

'I hope she will be pleased with England. Like Patrick in face, I mean.'

'We think her a good-looking girl.'

'Does she play? sing?'

'Some of our ballads.'

'She will delight my brother. John loves Irish ballads.'

A silence of long duration fell between them. She fancied he would like to sleep, and gently rose to slip away, that she might consult with Mrs. Lappett about putting up some tentcover. He asked her if she was going. 'Not home,' she said. His hand moved, but stopped. It seemed to have meant to detain her. She looked at a white fleece that came across the sun, desiring to conjure it to stay and shadow him. It sailed by. She raised her parasol.

His eyelids were shut, and she thought him asleep. Meditating on her unanswered question of Miss Kathleen's likeness to Patrick, Jane imagined a possibly greater likeness to her patient, and that he did not speak of his family's exclamations on the subject because of Kathleen's being so good-looking a girl. For if good-looking, a sister must resemble these handsome features here, quiescent to inspection in their marble outlines as a corse. So might he lie on the battle-field, with no one to watch over him!

While she watched, sitting close beside him to shield his head from the sunbeams, her heart began to throb before she well knew the secret of it. She had sight of a tear that grew big under the lashes of each of his eyelids, and rolled heavily. Her own eyes overflowed.

The fit of weeping was momentary, April's, a novelty with her. She accused her silly visions of having softened her. A hasty smoothing to right and left removed the traces; they were unseen; and when she ventured to look at him again there was no sign of fresh drops falling. His eyelids kept shut.

The arrival of her diurnal basket of provisions offered a refreshing intervention of the commonplace. Bright air had sharpened his appetite: he said he had been sure it would, and anticipated cheating the doctor of a part of the sentence which condemned him to lie on his back up to the middle of June, a log. Jane was hungry too, and they feasted together gaily, talking of Kathleen on her journey, her strange impressions and her way of proclaiming them, and of Patrick and where he might be now; ultimately of Captain Con and Mrs. Adister.

'He has broken faith with her,' Philip said sternly. 'She will have the right to tell him so. He never can be anything but a comic politician. Still he was bound to consult his wife previous to stepping before the public. He knows that he married a fortune.'

'A good fortune,' said Jane.

Philip acquiesced. 'She is an excellent woman, a model of uprightness; she has done him all the good in the world, and here is he deceiving her, lying—there is no other word: and one lie leads to another. When he married a fortune he was a successful adventurer. The compact was understood. His duty as a man of honour is to be true to his bond and serve the lady. Falseness to his position won't wash him clean of the title.'

Jane pleaded for Captain Con. 'He is chivalrously attentive to her.'

'You have read his letter,' Philip replied.

He crushed her charitable apologies with references to the letter.

'We are not certain that Mrs. Adister will object,' said she.

'Do you see her reading a speech of her husband's?' he remarked. Presently with something like a moan:

'And I am her guest!'

'Oh! pray, do not think Mrs. Adister will ever allow you to feel the lightest shadow...' said Jane.

'No; that makes it worse.'

Had this been the burden of his thoughts when those two solitary tears forced their passage? Hardly: not even in his physical weakness would he consent to weep for such a cause.

'I forgot to mention that Mrs. Adister has a letter from her husband telling her he has been called over to Ireland on urgent business,' she said.

Philip answered: 'He is punctilious.'

'I wish indeed he had been more candid,' Jane assented to the sarcasm.

'In Ireland he is agreeably surprised by the flattering proposal of a vacant seat, and not having an instant to debate on it, assumes the consent of the heavenliest wife in Christendom.'

Philip delivered the speech with a partial imitation of Captain Con addressing his wife on his return as the elected among the pure Irish party. The effort wearied him.

She supposed he was regretting his cousin's public prominence in the ranks of the malcontents. 'He will listen to you,' she said, while she smiled at his unwonted display of mimicry.

'A bad mentor for him. Antics are harmless, though they get us laughed at,' said Philip.

'You may restrain him from excesses.'

'Were I in that position, you would consider me guilty of greater than any poor Con is likely to commit.'

'Surely you are not for disunion?'

'The reverse. I am for union on juster terms, that will hold it fast.'

'But what are the terms?'

He must have desired to paint himself as black to her as possible. He stated the terms, which were hardly less than the affrighting ones blown across the Irish sea by that fierce party. He held them to be just, simply sensible terms. True, he spoke of the granting them as a sure method to rally all Ireland to an ardent love of the British flag. But he praised names of Irish leaders whom she had heard Mr. Rockney denounce for disloyal insolence: he could find excuses for them and their dupes—poor creatures, verily! And his utterances had a shocking emphasis. Then she was not wrong in her idea of the conspirator's head, her first impression of him!

She could not quit the theme: doing that would have been to be indifferent: something urged her to it.

'Are they really your opinions?'

He seemed relieved by declaring that they were.

'Patrick is quite free of them,' said she.

'We will hope that the Irish fever will spare Patrick. He was at a Jesuit college in France when he was wax. Now he's taking the world.'

'With so little of the Jesuit in him!'

'Little of the worst: a good deal of the best.'

'What is the best?'

'Their training to study. They train you to concentrate the brain upon the object of study. And they train you to accept service: they fit you for absolute service: they shape you for your duties in the world; and so long as they don't smelt a man's private conscience, they are model masters. Happily Patrick has held his own. Not the Jesuits would have a chance of keeping a grasp on Patrick! He'll always be a natural boy and a thoughtful man.'

Jane's features implied a gentle shudder.

'I shake a scarlet cloak to you?' said Philip.

She was directed by his words to think of the scarlet coat. 'I reflect a little on the substance of things as well,' she said. 'Would not Patrick's counsels have an influence?'

'Hitherto our Patrick has never presumed to counsel his elder brother.'

'But an officer wearing...'

'The uniform! That would have to be stripped off. There'd be an end to any professional career.'

'You would not regret it?'

'No sorrow is like a soldier's bidding farewell to flag and comrades. Happily politics and I have no business together. If the country favours me with active service I'm satisfied for myself. You asked me for my opinions: I was bound to give them. Generally I let them rest.'

Could she have had the temerity? Jane marvelled at herself.

She doubted that the weighty pair of tears had dropped for the country. Captain Con would have shed them over Erin, and many of them. Captain Philip's tone was too plain and positive: he would be a most practical unhistrionic rebel.

'You would countenance a revolt?' she said, striking at that extreme to elicit the favourable answer her tones angled for. And it was instantly:

'Not in arms.' He tried an explanation by likening the dissension to a wrangle in a civilised family over an unjust division of property.

And here, as he was marking the case with some nicety and difficulty, an itinerant barrel-organ crashed its tragic tale of music put to torture at the gate. It yelled of London to Jane, throttled the spirits of the woods, threw a smoke over the country sky, befouled the pure air she loved.

The instrument was one of the number which are packed to suit all English tastes and may be taken for a rough sample of the jumble of them, where a danceless quadrille-tune succeeds a suicidal Operatic melody and is followed by the weariful hymn, whose last drawl pert polka kicks aside. Thus does the poor Savoyard compel a rich people to pay for their wealth. Not without pathos in the abstract perhaps do the wretched machines pursue their revolutions of their factory life, as incapable of conceiving as of bestowing pleasure: a bald cry for pennies through the barest pretence to be agreeable but Jane found it hard to be tolerant of them out of London, and this one affecting her invalid and Mrs. Adister must be dismissed. Wayland was growling; he had to be held by the collar. He spied an objectionable animal. A jerky monkey was attached to the organ; and his coat was red, his kepi was blue; his tailor had rigged him as a military gentleman. Jane called to the farm-wife. Philip assured her he was not annoyed. Jane observed him listening, and by degrees she distinguished a maundering of the Italian song she had one day sung to Patrick in his brother's presence.

'I remember your singing that the week before I went to India,' said Philip, and her scarlet blush flooded her face.

'Can you endure the noise?' she asked him.

'Con would say it shrieks "murder." But I used to like it once.'

Mrs. Lappett came answering to the call. Her children were seen up the garden setting to one another with squared aprons, responsive to a livelier measure.

'Bless me, miss, we think it so cheerful!' cried Mrs. Lappett, and glanced at her young ones harmonious and out of mischief.

'Very well,' said Jane, always considerate for children. She had forgotten the racked Mrs. Adister.

Now the hymn of Puritanical gloom-the peacemaker with Providence performing devotional exercises in black bile. The leaps of the children were dashed. A sallow two or three minutes composed their motions, and then they jumped again to the step for lively legs. The similarity to the regimental band heading soldiers on the march from Church might have struck Philip.

'I wonder when I shall see Patrick!' he said, quickened in spite of himself by the sham sounds of music to desire changes and surprises.

Jane was wondering whether he could be a man still to brood tearfully over his old love.

She echoed him. 'And I! Soon, I hope.'

The appearance of Mrs. Adister with features which were the acutest critical summary of the discord caused toll to be paid instantly, and they beheld a flashing of white teeth and heard Italian accents. The monkey saluted militarily, but with painful suggestions of his foregone drilling in the ceremony.

'We are safe nowhere from these intrusions,' Mrs. Adister said; 'not on these hills!—and it must be a trial for the wretched men to climb them, that thing on their backs.'

'They are as accustomed to it as mountain smugglers bearing packs of contraband,' said Philip.

'Con would have argued him out of hearing before he ground a second note,' she resumed. 'I have no idea when Con returns from his unexpected visit to Ireland.'

'Within a fortnight, madam.'

'Let me believe it! You have heard from him? But you are in the air! exposed! My head makes me stupid. It is now five o'clock. The air begins to chill. Con will never forgive me if you catch a cold, and I would not incur his blame.'

The eyes of Jane and Philip shot an exchange.

'Anything you command, madam,' said Philip.

He looked up and breathed his heaven of fresh air. Jane pitied, she could not interpose to thwart his act of resignation. The farmer, home for tea, and a footman, took him between them, crutched, while Mrs. Adister said to Jane: 'The doctor's orders are positive:—if he is to be a man once more, he must rest his back and not use his legs for months. He was near to being a permanent cripple from that fall. My brother Edward had one like it in his youth. Soldiers are desperate creatures.'

'I think Mr. Adister had his fall when hunting, was it not?' said Jane.

'Hunting, my dear.'

That was rather different from a fall on duty before the enemy, incurred by severe exhaustion after sunstroke!...

Jane took her leave of Philip beside his couch of imprisonment in his room, promising to return in the early morning. He embraced her old dog Wayland tenderly. Hard men have sometimes a warm affection for dogs.

Walking homeward she likewise gave Wayland a hug. She called him 'dear old fellow,' and questioned him of his fondness for her, warning him not to be faithless ever to the mistress who loved him. Was not her old Wayland as good a protector as the footman Mrs. Adister pressed her to have at her heels? That he was!

Captain Con's behaviour grieved her. And it certainly revived an ancient accusation against his countrymen. If he cared for her so much, why had he not placed confidence in her and commissioned her to speak of his election to his wife? Irishmen will never be quite sincere!— But why had his cousin exposed him to one whom he greatly esteemed? However angry he might be with Con O'Donnell in his disapproval of the captain's conduct, it was not very considerate to show the poor man to her in his natural colours. Those words: 'The consolidation of the Union:' sprang up. She had a dim remembrance of words ensuing: 'ceremonies going at a funeral pace... on the highway to the solidest kind of union:'—Yes, he wrote: 'I leave you to...' And Captain Philip showed her the letter:

She perceived motives beginning to stir. He must have had his intention: and now as to his character!—Jane was of the order of young women possessing active minds instead of figured paste-board fronts, who see what there is to be seen about them and know what may be known instead of decorously waiting for the astonishment of revelations. As soon as she had asked herself the nature of the design of so honourable a man as Captain Philip in showing her his cousin's letter, her blood spun round and round, waving the reply as a torch; and the question of his character confirmed it.

But could he be imagined seeking to put her on her guard? There may be modesty in men well aware of their personal attractions: they can credit individual women with powers of resistance. He was not vain to the degree which stupefies the sense of there being weight or wisdom in others. And he was honour's own. By these lights of his character she read the act. His intention was... and even while she saw it accurately, the moment of keen perception was overclouded by her innate distrust of her claim to feminine charms. For why should he wish her to understand that he was no fortune-hunter and treated heiresses with greater reserve than ordinary women!

How could it matter to him?

She saw the tears roll. Tears of men sink plummet-deep; they find their level. The tears of such a man have more of blood than of water in them.—What was she doing when they fell? She was shading his head from the sun. What, then, if those tears came of the repressed desire to thank her with some little warmth? He was honour's own, and warmhearted Patrick talked of him as a friend whose heart was, his friend's. Thrilling to kindness, and, poor soul! helpless to escape it, he felt perhaps that he had never thanked her, and could not. He lay there, weak and tongue-tied: hence those two bright volumes of his condition of weakness.

So the pursuit of the mystery ended, as it had commenced, in confusion, but of a milder sort and partially transparent at one or two of the gates she had touched. A mind capable of seeing was twisted by a nature that would not allow of open eyes; yet the laden emotions of her nature brought her round by another channel to the stage neighbouring sight, where facts, dimly recognised for such—as they may be in truth, are accepted under their disguises, because disguise of them is needed by the bashful spirit which accuses itself of audaciousness in presuming to speculate. Had she asked herself the reason of her extended speculation, her foot would not have stopped more abruptly on the edge of a torrent than she on that strange road of vapours and flying lights. She did not; she sang, she sent her voice through the woods and took the splendid ring of it for an assurance of her peculiarly unshackled state. She loved this liberty. Of the men who had 'done her the honour,' not one had moved her to regret the refusal. She lived in the hope of simply doing good, and could only give her hand to a man able to direct and help her; one who would bear to be matched with her brother. Who was he? Not discoverable; not likely to be.

Therefore she had her freedom, an absolutely unflushed freedom, happier than poor Grace Barrow's. Rumour spoke of Emma Colesworth having a wing clipped. How is it that sensible women can be so susceptible? For, thought Jane, the moment a woman is what is called in love, she can give her heart no longer to the innocent things about her; she is cut away from Nature: that pure well-water is tasteless to her. To me it is wine!

The drinking of the pure well-water as wine is among the fatal signs of fire in the cup, showing Nature at work rather to enchain the victim than bid her daughter go. Jane of course meant the poet's 'Nature.' She did not reflect that the strong glow of poetic imagination is wanted to hallow a passionate devotion to the inanimate for this evokes the spiritual; and passionateness of any kind in narrower brains should be a proclamation to us of sanguine freshets not coming from a spiritual source. But the heart betraying deluded her. She fancied she had not ever been so wedded to Nature as on that walk through the bursting beechwoods, that sweet lonely walk, perfect in loneliness, where even a thought of a presence was thrust away as a desecration and images of souls in thought were shadowy.

Her lust of freedom gave her the towering holiday. She took the delirium in her own pure fashion, in a love of the bankside flowers and the downy edges of the young beech-buds fresh on the sprays. And it was no unreal love, though too intent and forcible to win the spirit from the object. She paid for this indulgence of her mood by losing the spirit entirely. At night she was a spent rocket. What had gone she could not tell: her very soul she almost feared. Her glorious walk through the wood seemed burnt out. She struck a light to try her poet on the shelf of the elect of earth by her bed, and she read, and read flatness. Not his fault! She revered him too deeply to lay it on him. Whose was it? She had a vision of the gulfs of bondage.

Could it be possible that human persons were subject to the spells of persons with tastes, aims, practices, pursuits alien to theirs? It was a riddle taxing her to solve it for the resistance to a monstrous iniquity of injustice, degrading her conception of our humanity. She attacked it in the abstract, as a volunteer champion of our offended race. And Oh! it could not be. The battle was won without a blow.

Thereupon came glimpses of the gulfs of bondage, delicious, rose-enfolded, foreign; they were chapters of soft romance, appearing interminable, an endless mystery, an insatiable thirst for the mystery. She heard crashes of the opera-melody, and despising it even more than the wretched engine of the harshness, she was led by it, tyrannically led a captive, like the organ-monkey, until perforce she usurped the note, sounded the cloying tune through her frame, passed into the vulgar sugariness, lost herself.

And saying to herself: This is what moves them! she was moved. One thrill of appreciation drew her on the tide, and once drawn from shore she became submerged. Why am I not beautiful, was her thought. Those voluptuous modulations of melting airs are the natural clothing of beautiful women. Beautiful women may believe themselves beloved. They are privileged to believe, they are born with the faith.

Printed in Great Britain
by Amazon